ANGEL OF THE UNDERGROUND

A NOVEL BY
DAVID ANDREAS

ODDITIES KJB

This is a work of fiction. All names, characters, places, and incidents are a product of the author's imagination. Any resemblance to real events or persons, living or dead, is entirely coincidental.

Published by Akashic Books
©2018 David Andreas
Illustrations ©2018 David Andreas

ISBN: 978-1-61775-635-1
eISBN: 978-1-61775-636-8
Library of Congress Control Number: 2017951365

Kaylie Jones Books Oddities
c/o Akashic Books
Twitter: @AkashicBooks
Facebook: AkashicBooks
info@akashicbooks.com
www.akashicbooks.com

For Alice Cooper

To forgive is divine,
but vengeance is mine.

—Alice Cooper

CHAPTER I

Three children recently checked out of the Hartman Catholic Group Home in unspeakable ways. Their murders are amongst the worst ever committed on Long Island. I haven't blamed God for not protecting them, but I am coming to believe His ways are as mysterious as they are malicious.

Kim Reidy was the first to die. Five weeks ago, she disappeared from the playground behind our church following mass. One child later said Kim followed a voice into the woods, but the alleged source was never seen. A daylong search in the nearby vicinity came up empty. Later that night, the police found Kim's body in a weeded lot past a dead-end street two miles from our home. Only minor details regarding her cause of death were relayed to the media, but a witness leaked a cell phone photo showing her corpse. Blood was smeared across the white unicorn of her pink shirt and her left eye was missing.

My social worker, a stiff woman named Clara, grumbles as she navigates her Buick Regal over a deep pothole. She hasn't said a word to me during the ordeal of peddling me to a new family. I doubt she even knows my name, since she constantly refers me to others as the "older female subject." Her job is to take me from the group home, deliver me to a charitable family, and go about her business with the two other surviving kids. I feel as though I'm a task to her, and not a cause for concern.

Eleven days after Kim's body was found, Bryan Nabatova went missing from his bedroom sometime between his eight o'clock bedtime and dawn. The sliced screen on his ground floor window suggested an intruder with specific intentions. Detectives found his carcass, dressed in his favorite fire truck pajamas, stuffed in the steel base of a train trestle and partially covered with lava rocks. As with Kim, clues to the killer's identity were either unknown or withheld. The police informed the public that they were dealing with someone who had a personal investment in the crimes, as suggested by their high levels of violence. One particular trait tied them to the same culprit; Bryan's left eye had also been extracted.

My social worker pulls up before my temporary house so abruptly the tires vibrate. The place is white with green shutters. I close my eyes, grasp the gold crucifix charm that hangs from my neck, and whisper a prayer for strength. I assume the door will open for me, and Clara will escort me to my new lodgings, but when I open my eyes I find her standing outside checking her watch.

I reluctantly step out with my red suitcase, from crisp air conditioning to savage humidity. The butterflies in my stomach are waging war on each other. Clara hurries onto a blacktop driveway that branches off to a concrete stoop. I walk behind her at a much slower pace, happy to notice my right shoelace coming undone. "One second, please," I say, to which Clara heaves a sigh. I kneel to tie my sneaker and pray for the will to carry on.

The third death that led to the group home's sudden evacuation occurred within the house itself. Chris Myrow was claimed during the night. I had the displeasure of finding him while rounding up the kids for breakfast. He was hog tied with the same blue jump rope he often got in trouble for using indoors. A Nerf football was stuffed down his mouth and exposed through a slit in his throat. The sheet beneath him, once colorful with blue and orange triangles, had turned various shades of black and red. On the wall beside him, under a tacked up poster of Spider-Man, were the white-jelly remnants of his smeared left eye.

Once news of Chris' murder broke, our already tense group home became increasingly hectic. The phone never stopped ringing, spectators hung around on the street day and night, and news reporters set up camp on a neighbor's lawn to film our home around the clock. Police frequently stopped in to check on us, and even arrested someone who refused to stop taking pictures from the property line.

Instead of relocating the three survivors to another Catholic group home, our director decided to transfer us to separate foster homes across Long Island. We were picked up with relative ease. Married couples came and went, interacting with us under the watchful eyes of lawyers and social workers. Peter Heffernan and Amanda Czark were chosen on the first day, while I had to wait until the following afternoon. At fifteen, by far the oldest, I didn't warrant the sympathy showered upon those deemed too young to defend themselves.

While out in the backyard throwing a baseball against a pitch back, Sister Alice, wearing an
old-fashioned skirt suit, called me in to meet a couple who'd come to see me. In the living room, my
social worker and a suited lawyer were sitting on our
three-cushioned couch. Across from them, on a much
smaller love seat, sat Barry and Lori Grantham.
Barry looked as though he was smuggling pillows under his shirt and down the legs of his slacks. Lori, on
the other hand, was splinter thin. She sat compressed in
the tight groove between her husband and the arm of
the couch wearing a look of complete displeasure.

Barry's face, shrunken in the midst of his cheeks,
beamed when he offered his hand to me and said,
"You must be Robin."

I accepted his damp palm and replied, "Yes, sir.
I'm pleased to meet you."

He shook my hand a little too hard, which strained
my shoulder socket, and tilted his head while staring
into my eyes. "Are those contacts? No eyes are that
blue."

"They're all mine."

I recovered my hand from Barry and offered it
to Lori. She touched my palm with the tips of her
fingers. Her eyes never rose above the button of my
jeans. I uneasily backed into Sister Alice as the lawyer

said to her, "We'll need a moment with you in private, Sister."

Sister Alice turned me to the back door and whispered, "I'll put in some good words."

She came outside twenty minutes later and explained that the couple had taken an interest in my high grades and good behavior, but said I shouldn't get my hopes up since the blessed don't always get what they deserve. A phone call later that day indicated they had decided to take me in after all. Sister Alice and I packed as much as we could into my meager suitcase, making sure to include my prized possessions: my Bible, wooden crucifix, and baseball mitt.

I rise from tying my sneaker and find Clara twirling her hand to speed me up. When I approach the front door, she steps aside and gives me the nerve-wracking honor of introducing myself to whomever might answer. I walk up the three steps and press a glowing doorbell to summon the first player in my new and remorseless life.

CHAPTER II

Worried no one is eager to meet me, I ring the doorbell a second time. As I gear up to knock, a storm door opens. An old man in brown slacks and a blue checkered shirt glances outside. His eyes repeatedly blink as though he just woke up. When he finds me I pay him an apologetic smile.

The old man opens the screen door outward while saying, "Oh, good, you're here! Come in out of that heat!" I step inside to the cool air, but Clara follows no closer than the second step. The old man says to her, "Would you like to come in for some lemonade?"

"Thanks, but no," Clara replies, and hands him a manila envelope. "Call the numbers provided if you have any problems or questions about her." Without saying so much as a goodbye or good luck to me, she walks away, adjusting her tight skirt. The old man closes both doors, shutting out everything I'm familiar with.

I set my suitcase down beside a sofa and clasp my hands over my stomach. My frenzied butterflies are disrupting my bladder. I don't want to ruin the old man's first impression of me by having to go to the bathroom, so I try to will the nerves down by taking deep breaths through my nose.

The old man smiles at me with perfectly white teeth, while his face crinkles upward toward a scalp full of brown spots. "Would you like a glass of lemonade?" he asks. "I'd hate to see it go to waste on a day like this."

Running dry, I say, "I'd love some."

"Great! Have a seat right over there and I'll go get us some." While he shuffles into a kitchen on bowed legs, I approach a wooden chair that's resting near a green recliner. A small television tucked in a wooden entertainment center is showing a black-and-white documentary about a war. The volume is muted. On a shelf above the TV are an assortment of remote controls, framed pictures of strangers, and the receiver to a child's monitor. The red light is glowing, but the speaker emits no sounds.

I sit on the edge of the chair facing a dining room. Beneath a frosted chandelier is a shiny oak table surrounded by five upholstered chairs. A matching hutch with glass doors is filled with china plates, crystal glasses, and wedding trinkets. A door at the far right of the room has a handwritten sign that reads, *BEWARE!*

The old man carries in a green plastic tray with a clear pitcher of iced lemonade on one side, and two stacked glasses on the other. His tongue worms out from his mouth as though leading the way. He places the tray on an end table while sliding back a lamp with a flowery shade. After separating the glasses, he lifts the pitcher with a considerable amount of strain and pours them both full. He hands me the first glass with a wobbly hand, and sits down in the recliner with the other glass. Upon landing, one of his hips pops and causes him to groan. He smiles through the pain, and when it's clear he's not injured I say, "This is a very nice house, sir."

"Please, call me Nathan." He toasts his glass to me and takes a delicate sip. I down three big swallows, which soothe my parched throat. Nathan watches me with gratification. "Looks like the weather has gotten to you."

"Among other things."

"Did you know we have a pool?"

Sister Alice had mentioned as much. She also brought up the two boys who were adopted into the family, and said their ages were close to mine. "Will the other kids mind sharing with me?"

He leans forward and sternly says, "If those two give you any problems, you come see me."

I pat a hand over my crucifix charm to show him I'm protected and say, "I guarantee they won't bring me down."

Nathan laughs so abruptly his upper teeth shift off their brackets and project from his mouth. To pretend I don't notice, I look over the wall décor, which mainly consists of a large painting of geese flying over a wooded stream at dawn. Strangely, there isn't a single mark of religion anywhere. I don't expect every house to live up to the group home's standards, but most places I've visited at least have a cross here or there.

"You're pretty secretive in your spiritual beliefs."

Nathan bites his dentures back into place, hisses up drool, and says, "I'm afraid those days are long gone. We got rid of God years ago." My stomach bursts into flames, incinerating my lemonade-coated butterflies. "I'm surprised no one told you."

"A lot was left out in the rush." I had assumed I would go from one Catholic house to another, but understood the importance of leaving an active crime scene regardless of anyone's association with the Almighty. I loosen my grip on the lemonade glass, so I don't end up with a handful of wet shards, and force a contented smile.

"You've nothing to worry about. We won't get in the way of your practices, no matter how purposeless they may be." Nathan reaches over to the end table for an orange pill box shaped like a seashell, and extracts a white capsule from inside. "As much as I hate to cut our conversation short, the doc's got me on a tight schedule with these little ditties, and they tend to knock me out cold." He takes the pill with his lemonade, rubs his larynx with an index finger to will the "ditty" down, and coarsely says, "Not that you wanted to keep an old man company all day."

"Is the couple that found me home?"

"They'll be back from work around seven." He stands and pats my head. "Let me show you out back. The sooner you let those boys warm up to you the better."

I put my glass down on the tray and follow Nathan into a kitchen that's carpeted beneath a corner table but tiled everywhere else. He opens a wooden door that leads out to a garage, where gardening and lawn equipment are strewn near a back wall. A workbench is littered with tools, pipes, and multicolored wires. Two BMX bikes lie on the oil spotted concrete.

A screened storm door on our right leads to the backyard, where I can hear the sounds of a baseball slapping into separate gloves. I think to get mine, but don't want to make Nathan wait on my account. Not with his tight schedule and all.

I step outside onto a concrete patio that holds a picnic table, matching benches, and a charcoal grill. To my far right is an above ground pool coupled with an unpainted wooden deck. The surrounding lawn has more crabgrass than regular grass, widespread brown patches, and a ton of anthills. Further back, beyond a long two-post fence, the boys are throwing a baseball back and forth. One boy stands in front of a wire-enclosed garden, the other a homemade swing set where four wooden benches hang on heavy chains.

I march through the damp heat, passing a white aluminum shed with crooked green doors, and make eye contact with the boy in front of the garden. He's bony and has dark circles beneath his eyes. I smile at him, but he rolls his eyes away and seems to snarl. I alter my direction toward the other boy, who looks slightly older and has a fuller figure. After catching a fastball that pops into his glove, he notices me and offers a thin smile, though his eyes remain cheerless. I can't tell if he's nervous to meet me or agitated that I'm interrupting them, but when I stop at the fence he says in a friendly tone, "Robin, right?"

"That's me," I reply. "Sorry, but I forgot your names."

"I'm Dennis. That's Jeremy."

"Pleased to meet you," Jeremy says, "now go back inside and fuck yourself! This isn't a good month to be seen with any of you zealots from that death trap!"

Though I've had plenty of practice in school dealing with kids not wanting anything to do with me, thanks to my religious background and outdated dresses, Jeremy's words and their heated tone anger me to the core. The Granthams are supposed to offer compassionate safety, not mindless banter from bullies.

Dennis taps his mitt on my shoulder. "Don't listen to a word he says. He doesn't like anybody who isn't him."

"I brought my own glove," I say. "Can I play?"

"Are you any good?"

I hold out my hand for the ball. Dennis drops it into my palm. I crawl through the fence posts and, after a quick windup, throw heat at Jeremy. In trying too hard to show off my speed, the ball sinks and hits the dirt. Jeremy could have taken a step forward to keep me from looking like a fool, but he lets the ball skip past him and roll against the garden. He issues a demeaning snort and says, "Who taught you how to throw? An altar boy with a sore bunghole?"

"Her velocity's up there," Dennis says.

"Big deal! She could have queefed with better location."

Nobody on ESPN ever used such a term to describe a pitch, but since it came from Jeremy, I figure it's best to ignore what he means.

Dennis steps in front of me, as if to purposely block my view of his adoptive brother. "Did you see your room yet? Barry made me paint it. Not that I minded."

"Not yet," I reply.

He takes off his glove, looks back at Jeremy who's facing us in a pitching stance, and tells him, "I'm showing her to her room. If that ball comes near us, you'll eat it."

Jeremy readjusts himself and darts the ball directly into the garden, snapping a wooden post that had been supporting green tomatoes. Unfazed, Dennis heads toward the house as though he's seen this type of behavior before.

I follow Dennis through the kitchen and into the dining room, where my suitcase is leaning against the door with the warning sign. Nathan, who's snoring in his chair, must have placed it there before conking out. Though I was expecting Dennis to show me to a room upstairs, once he opens the door and flips on a light switch, I curiously follow him down a flight of

twelve wooden steps. At the bottom is a finished basement where circular lights are embedded in a ceiling
of sheet rock. The floor has light blue carpeting, the
walls are paneled, and the odor is a blend of fresh
paint, stale air, and mildew.

Across the hall from two closed doors is an open
room that Dennis presents to me with open hands. I
peek inside with gratification. The area is small but
perfectly suitable for a short stay. The furnishings are
white, the walls pink, and the carpet matches the hallway. There's nothing in the way of décor, but I don't
mind because I don't plan on staying long enough to
embellish the space.

"If you need anything," Dennis says, "I'm not far."

"Thank you," I reply. "The paint looks great, by
the way." He turns red while going to his room.

I set my suitcase on the bed and retrieve my crucifix; a foot long, wooden cross that supports a silver
Jesus. I kneel before a rectangular window that has
no curtain, and recite three "Our Fathers" for the orphans who perished and would no longer face new
experiences, no matter how uncomfortable or uncer-
tain they might be.

While putting away what little clothes I have in a
closet with a mirrored inner door, I find a blue bikini
hanging on a plastic hanger with the price tag still

attached. I hold it up to myself while facing my reflection, and though I'm not sure if I could ever wear something so skimpy in front of two boys, I'm happy to have been given a welcome present. Any calm I feel is cut short when someone pounds on my door in rapid succession, causing my heart to leap into my throat. I spin around and find Jeremy showing me his middle fingers. "I heard you prissy religious freaks like Slayer," he says. "Well, today's your lucky day!"

After he slams his bedroom door shut, a radio goes on full blast. What he plays sounds like an orchestration from Hell. The fury of squealing guitars and rapid drumbeats are only outmatched by a despondent singer who ultimately shouts, "*GOD HATES US ALL!*" I close my door, which cuts out everything but the pummeling bass.

With nobody familiar to keep me company, and exhausted from hardly sleeping last night, I lie on the bed and try taking a nap. Between the sun reflecting off the window's white lacquer surface, and a mind that won't stop reminding me that the killer has not been apprehended, I can't come close to falling under. To pass time, I read through my Bible for stories of patience, of which there are plenty. Abraham was made to wait years before God would grant him a promised child; Joseph waited a lengthy amount of

time for God to make him leader of his people; and
Simeon was not allowed to die until he witnessed the
birth of the Messiah. By comparison, catching the
murderer is something I shouldn't expect the police
to do anytime soon.

Around six o'clock, a loud knock sounds on my
door. Before I can invite anyone in, Barry opens it up
and leans inside. He's wearing black slacks, a white
dress shirt, and a navy blue vest with a King Kullen
name tag. In a voice loud enough to compete with
Jeremy's still-blaring music he says, "If this noise becomes a problem, you let me know!"

As irritating as I find Jeremy's musical taste, I
don't want to get him in trouble, so I tilt my head
toward a shrugging shoulder and say, "I'll be all
right."

"You like pizza?"

"I do."

"Then come on up. We got pepperoni!" Barry
pushes himself off the door frame and excitedly hurries away. I hope for his sake he slows down before
reaching the stairs, as it's well known people his size
are destined for early heart attacks.

In the dining room, Nathan is siting at one head
of the table and staring groggily at a glass of lemonade. When he notices me, he pulls out the seat closest

to himself and pats the cushion. I sit next to him and ask, "How was your nap?"

"I had the most wonderful dream," he replies, inspecting his wrinkled hands. "I won't bore you with the details, but I haven't felt that young in years." When I motion to ask what he means, Barry carries in two pizza boxes from the kitchen. Lori follows with a stack of plates and napkins. When she catches me looking at her, her lips stretch into an artificial smile and her eyes dart away.

Barry sets the boxes down, opens the top one, and starts digging out a slice with his bare fingers. My stomach sours. Sister Alice always uses a spatula, even after she washes her hands. Barry drops the slice onto a plate and slides it down to me. I guide it to Nathan, since the patriarch deserves to eat first. Nathan leans in toward me and says, "Should the doctor ask, this never happened." He pays me a wink, so I pay him one back.

Barry passes another plate to me, licks sauce off two of his fingers, and pries out a slice for Lori. Her curled upper lip suggests she has no intentions of eating anything violated by her own husband's spit. After piling up three slices on his plate, Barry sits next to me with his legs so far apart his left knee presses against my right thigh. "*Mangia!*" he says.

Before anyone can take their first bite, I couple my hands in prayer, bow my head, and say aloud, "Bless us O Lord, and these Thy gifts which we are about to receive from Thy bounty through Christ our Lord. Amen."

I look up to six bewildered eyes. Nobody says anything, which makes me wonder if I've offended them by speaking of things Nathan referred to as *purposeless*. In the midst of their overlong silence, Nathan finally says, "Eat up," which eases some discomfort.

Barry folds his slice down the middle and bites off half. He chews like the Brahman bull I once saw eating hay at the Bald Hill Fair. I pick up my slice and nibble on the tip. I have a knack for getting sauce on my shirts, and don't want to look like a slob during our first gathering. Luckily, Barry starts talking to me, which takes away the pressure from having to eat. "The nun mentioned you two are baseball fans," he says.

"We sure are," I reply.

"If you play your cards right, I'll let you watch the game with me after dinner."

"That sounds great. They're playing the Marlins and their ace is starting."

Barry laughs so hard he has to spit out a soggy wad of dough to catch his breath. Lori looks away in disgust. "Why in the world would I want to watch those losers? Around here, young lady, we follow the Yankees."

I swallow hard to keep the pizza bite from running back up my throat. Sister Alice and I have spent the bulk of the past three summers watching baseball, but our favorite team is the Mets. She made it perfectly clear that the Yankees organization is in league with Lucifer to have been permitted so much steroid and salary abuse throughout the past few decades. "Actually, I'm feeling a bit run down. I'd like to call Sister Alice, and then see about going to bed."

Lori snickers. Barry turns red while his head descends into his chins. I've obviously hurt his feelings for refusing his invitation in front of others, but I feel worse realizing the Mets pregame show is about to begin. Sister Alice and I would be putting the kids in their pajamas and reading them their bedtime stories. Afterward, we'd make popcorn and chocolate milk and settle in just in time for the first pitch.

When dinner comes to a close, I excuse myself into the kitchen and call the group home from a wall phone near the fridge. It's been too long since I've heard Sister Alice's voice, but I'll have to wait longer as I'm met with our answering machine. I'd like to think she's watching the Mets with the volume too high, but I'm afraid she's sitting by herself after another joyless day, wondering what she did wrong, and how all this could have happened when her pieties should have kept the devil out of our sanctuary. To hopefully lessen her pains, I leave a quick message letting her know I'm doing okay and I'm thinking about her.

I head downstairs with the intention of sleeping out the rest of the day, even though it's barely nine o'clock, but I haven't been alone in darkness since the children were taken. Sister Alice let us bunk in her room at night, and visiting patrons from our church community were always around during the day. With nobody here to distract me from the pain, I cry harder than I have since the first child was claimed. When a gentle knock sounds on my door, I wipe away tears and tell whomever it is to come in. The door opens a crack, letting in a beam of hallway light. "Were you sleeping?" Dennis asks.

"Not even close," I reply.

"Do you like horror movies?"

"Does *Casper* count?"

"If you're in Huggies. I'm putting one on for you if you're up for it." In need of a diversion, and eager to make friends of strangers, I swing my feet off the bed, hop up, and follow Dennis to his room. I abruptly stop in his doorway when noticing his decorations with quiet repulsion. The walls are cloaked with posters and magazine pages of horror movie villains and victims. Toys of madmen and monsters stand on anything with a flat surface. Five shelving units hold dozens of movies, all of which have titles that insinuate death and torment. Plus, there's no place for me to sit. Jeremy has the bed, Dennis claims a soft computer chair, and the floor is covered with dirty clothes.

Jeremy, outstretching his arms and legs to take up every inch of the mattress, says to me, "Take your holy ass to the carpet!" Dennis moves aside a pile of clothes with his foot, revealing a circular patch of carpeting.

I sit on my knees and say, "What are we watching?"

"Considering what you've been through," Dennis replies, "I'll start you off with something tame." He hands me the DVD box for *Child's Play 2*, where a living doll is holding a gigantic pair of scissors over the spring neck of a frightened jack-in-the-box. Though I'm in no mood to view anything immoral, I don't want to turn him down and appear as though I don't appreciate his offer, so I prepare myself for another new experience and sit Indian style against the foot of the bed.

At the beginning of *Child's Play 2*, a boy named Andy is taken in by a couple that cares for foster kids. Not long in, Chucky, a three-foot doll possessed by the spirit of a serial killer, hunts Andy down for whatever they squabbled over in the first film. Unfortunately, nobody believes that a doll could cause so many problems, so Andy is left to fend for himself. I feel relief that my first day in a new home is going better than Andy's.

Though I'm not accustomed to R-rated movies, *Child's Play 2* does offer warnings of violent mayhem, mainly through changes in music, which allow me to cover my eyes. Between the slits in my fingers I catch glimpses of an electrocution, a suffocation, and Chucky beating a school teacher to death with a yardstick. I make a sign of the cross after each murder, even though I can easily tell each death is staged. People don't get blown through windows because of small doses of electricity, a doll could never muster enough strength to suffocate anyone with a plastic bag, and no yardstick I ever held could pulverize a human without breaking.

Dennis and Jeremy don't seem to care about the implausibilities. They laugh during the murders and find amusement in watching people die. Jeremy, taking disrespect of the victims further, taunts the characters in their agony. He even cries out in rage during the finale, when Andy gets the best of Chucky by blowing him up.

When the film ends, I sit up on my knees, which

brings relief to my stinging feet, and lean sideways against the bed. "That wasn't exactly scary," I say.

"The first one was," Dennis replies, "but there's only so much tension you can wring out of plastic."

"Are there others? Seems a stretch to think Chucky could come back without a head."

"Only one way to find out. Are you up for Part Three?" Though watching humans die before their time doesn't thrill me, I'd rather deal with a killer doll than the cold darkness of my unfamiliar room.

When the boys call it a night, I have no choice but to go to bed and face my feelings alone. Whenever thoughts of death creep into my mind, I overshadow them with lighter memories of the deceased, such as the time Brian yelled at a chair because he dropped his toy when bumping into it; or the time Kim came home from preschool covered in paint because she preferred her shirt to canvas; or the time Chris insisted on dressing himself and came out of his room with his bumblebee underwear outside his pants. I can't say these thoughts make me happy, but they somehow lessen the horror of their deaths and allow exhaustion to catch up to me.

CHAPTER III

I awaken in the morning to pulsating heat against my back. I half-expect to find my roommate, Amanda, sleeping beside me, but the snoring sounds are too deep for a three-year-old. I look over my shoulder and find a bald, blemished scalp. I slither onto the floor, land hard on my right hip, and stare at Nathan with wide eyes. Still sound asleep, he rolls over facing me. His lips are stuck to his dry teeth, which makes him look like a skeleton veiled in tight skin.

A frantic voice sounds upstairs. I crawl to the hallway for a listen and hear Lori say, "Dad! Enough of this shit! Where are you?" I hurry up to the dining room, where Lori stops short and looks me over as though I'm interrupting her for no good reason. "Can I help you with something?"

"He's in my room," I reply.

"Isn't that nice? We've been going crazy up here while you two are having a fucking tea party?"

Before I can explain what's actually happening, she brushes past me and heads to the basement. I follow her with the hope that finding Nathan asleep will lead to an apology for chastising me with profanity, but when she sees Nathan she simply mutters, "Tell Barry to come in. He's out back."

Sure enough, Barry is leaning inside the aluminum shed. When he retracts himself and notices me he offers a quizzical gaze.

"He's downstairs," I say, "in my bed."

Barry places his hands on my shoulders and says, "You'll have to forgive him. He's not all there in the head and tends to forget where he is." He leads me to the garage with a hand on my back. "I wouldn't worry. He's far from a threat."

I give Barry the benefit of the doubt, but I don't say a word. I don't know about Nathan's health conditions, and can't feel too upset since he didn't do anything but sleep. Sister Alice says life is full of unplanned discomforts, so I forgive him as I expect Sister Alice would.

When Barry heads downstairs to gather his father, I find something of interest in a lidless kitchen garbage pail. Beneath a wet coffee filter is the latest *Newsday*. On the cover is a photo of Detective Morris, the policeman who spoke to me when I found Bryan's savaged body. While Nathan is taken upstairs, I slip the paper under my shirt and take it down to my room.

The main article clarifies what I already know. The police department has yet to disclose any clues or leads that might tie the murders to a suspect. Detective Morris is under public scrutiny for his inability to set anyone at ease. Answering "no comment" to almost every question is angering the already frightened community. Sales of guns, home security systems, and guard dogs have spiked over the past few weeks. Citizens are begging for a new detective to take on the case, as they find Morris wholly incompetent.

I think they're too hard on him. When we met he appeared concerned for my well-being; he told me I had witnessed a scene more brutal than any he's ever encountered before. At one point he excused himself to the bathroom, where he must have cried since he came out with swollen, bloodshot eyes. He promised me he'd catch the killer by any means necessary, but those means are eluding him.

After flipping through the rest of the paper, which ends with the Mets' three game losing streak, I call the group home and hang up on a busy signal. I head out back to see what the boys are up to and find Dennis in the pool. As I approach, Jeremy rises from the depths and blows water from his nose. He then says

to me: "Why the long face, slut? Couldn't get the gee-
zer off?" He laughs hard, but the sound doesn't relate
to humor. My eyes start to burn as tears fill the ducts.
Crying, even in the most minimal sense, often feeds
the wretchedness of people like Jeremy, so I look into
a sandy foot bath near the pool and try not to blink.

Dennis bobs closer to me and leans his arms
against the aluminum ledge. "Ignore him," he says,
"no one else thinks it's funny. Nathan has issues." I
look at him with appreciation just as Jeremy slides
an arm's length of cold water at me. My breath is immediately seized. Jeremy laughs so hard he begins to
choke. Undeserving of such treatment, I return downstairs, drop face first into my pillow, and don't expect
to hear from anyone until dinner.

At half past two, a light knock sounds on my
door, to which I reply, "Come in."

Dennis enters and closes the door behind himself,
probably so he can be heard over Jeremy's heavy
metal. "I'm heading out for a bit," he says. "Jeremy
will probably blast music the rest of the day. The pool
is all yours."

"Where are you going?"

"A place you're not allowed to go to. We were
told not to bring you anywhere."

"I'm not a prisoner. And I can't sit still without

thinking horrible thoughts about those kids. I need to get out of here." I look directly into his forlorn hazel eyes and clasp my hands. "*Please?*"

Dennis bites his upper lip while bouncing his head from side to side, then says in surrender, "It's only two miles away. If we hurry we can make it back before anyone knows you left."

I stand up and put on my Keds.

Though Jeremy is screaming along to his music, Dennis says he has a sense for knowing when something fun is happening without him, so we creep up to the garage and quietly wheel out the two bicycles. "You can take mine," Dennis says, "I'll use his."

Their bikes are nearly identical, and only slightly different than the one I grew up with. The top crossbar doesn't dip and the brakes aren't pedal operated, but I'm sure I'll adapt. I'm getting used to adapting.

Dennis initially rides hard and puts twenty yards between us, but when we reach a safe distance from the house he slows down so I can catch up. When side-by-side I ask, "Where are we going?"

"To the greatest place in creation," he replies.

"Can you be more specific?"

"Can I ask you something personal first?"

"Let me guess, how did I become an orphan?"

"I was wondering about something darker. You

come from a place named after a priest where kids were killed, yet I saw you sign the cross three times last night. I'm not sure I'd still worship the one who let that happen."

"God didn't kill anyone."

"He also didn't catch anyone."

I don't know how to respond because his point has been bothering me too. That vulnerable children were murdered is troubling enough, but that the murderer continues to roam free doesn't seem fair. Changing the subject I ask, "Where are you taking me?"

"My sanctuary." He gives me a wink and peddles faster. I keep pace, but allow him to take the lead when we reach a busy highway with a narrow sidewalk. Dennis leads me to an area where two lanes become four, the traffic lights multiply, and the speed limit increases. Sister Alice would forbid me to go anywhere near such a dangerous area, but I feel safe with Dennis. He seems to have made the trip many times before, and never does anything rash like cross a street without looking both ways, or ride through lanes that have green lights.

When we stop at an intersection and wait for traffic to pass, the windless heat catches up to me. We must have traveled well over a mile, and I can only hope our destination is near, as the sun is boiling

me toward a stroke. After reaching a stretch that's
clogged with fast food restaurants, car dealerships,
and private businesses, we coast into a parking lot
that contains a small row of mom and pop stores.
One of them is called 112 Video World. We climb off
our bikes and lean them against the front window.
Dennis chains them together, wipes sweat off his forehead with his sleeve, and opens the door for me.

I step into the cold wonder of air conditioning
with a massive sigh of relief. Dennis has an equal reaction, but I don't think it's related to the temperature
dip. His sanctuary consists of rental movies that are
packed top to bottom on wide shelving units. Pack-
aged toys, comic books, and movie memorabilia cover every wall and ledge. The place looks like his room,
only bigger.

A flat screen television is airing a movie where one
boy is helping another out from a pit of pint-sized
creatures, but Dennis has no interest in it. He puts
his hands on my shoulders and steers me toward the
DVD horror section.

"I didn't think this many movies existed," I say.
"Have you seen them all?"

"Don't I wish," he replies.

A young woman in a blue flannel shirt and yellow
sweatpants walks out from a back room with a box

of receipt paper. For some reason she's barefoot. She playfully nudges Dennis when passing him and says, "Anything specific today?"

"Nah. Just showing Robin your holy establishment."

"Don't let him warp you too much," the clerk says to me. When she walks behind the counter and starts fiddling with the receipt machine, I step closer to Dennis who's squatting before the C titles.

"How do you figure out which ones to pick?" I ask.

"I start with something random and build a double feature," he replies. "Two with 'massacre' in the title, two with meat cleavers on the cover, that kind of thing."

"What's today's theme?"

"I don't know. What mood are you in?"

"A sad one. Can any of these change that?"

"You know what always puts a smile on my face?"

"Hopefully not *Chopping Mall* or *Christmas Evil*."

"*Chopping Mall* is awesome, but I meant this." He hands me a box for a movie called *C.H.U.D*. The cover has a monster with bright eyes climbing out of a sewer. "The sequel's called *Bud the Chud*, but it bites the big one so we'll have to look for something else that's city or sewer related."

I point out a box that has a screaming face stretched over a city skyline. "How about *City of Blood*?" Dennis looks over the cover, and approves by placing it on top of *C.H.U.D.*

After close to a half-hour of watching Dennis scrutinize half the alphabet, we leave with a bag of four rentals. During the trip home, I feel confident that bonding with Dennis will lead to some outside activities along the lines of playing catch or going in the pool. I don't bring up either, as I plan to ask him about each during whichever movie we watch first. When we arrive back at his house, however, Dennis's joyful appearance vanishes when he sees a brown SUV parked crookedly in the driveway. Chunky rubber strips lead from the street to the back tires.

"Shit," Dennis mutters, "Barry's home."

While we're climbing off our bikes near the garage, Barry erupts from the front door and storms toward us. Despite his size, he moves awfully fast. Dennis, with no time to react defensively, is seized by his left ear and slapped in the gut. He crumples forward and coughs up a wad of phlegm that he spits on the lawn.

Barry points directly at me and says, "You go inside!" Stunned, I forget how to move. I try to think of a way to keep his temper from worsening, but am afraid I'm what set him off to begin with. I am, after all, supposed to remain hidden. "I'll deal with you in a minute, Robin! Now please, get in the house!"

Jeremy opens the front door and says, "You heard the man! Get your bike stealing ass in here!" Barry attacks Dennis with an array of open handed punches. Dennis grunts as he takes the hits. I press my palms against my ears and start humming, but I can still hear Jeremy's shrill laughter as he follows me into the living room. Not long after, Dennis fumes inside and heads straight for the basement. He rips open the door and slams it behind himself hard enough to make the chandelier swing back and forth.

Barry, sweaty and out of breath, enters with the video store bag. He peeks inside and says, "What the hell is a C.H.U.D.?"

"Cannibalistic Humanoid Underground Dweller," Jeremy says while snatching the bag. "Let me see what else they rented." He too goes downstairs, but closes the door gently.

Barry stands before me and puts his hands on his hips. I can't bring myself to look him in the eye. Even though Dennis did something wrong on my account, he didn't have to go through a beating by someone twice his size. Sister Alice has nonviolent ways of reprimanding us, and makes it clear that no person should ever physically harm another, since every con-flict in the world could be resolved with dialogue.

"I'm sorry," Barry says, "but he knew bringing you out in public is a bad idea. I specifically said—"

"Sit down, son," Nathan rasps from his chair. "The doc warned you about that heart."

Barry drops down on the couch and sinks deep into the cushions. He maneuvers himself forward and props his elbows on his knees. "The point in taking you in is so the guy killing everyone doesn't know where you are."

"I made the decision to go," I say.

"Honey, words could never describe the severity of your situation." I nod in partial agreement, since my traveling through town in broad daylight, despite my need for distraction, was actually dangerous, but I can't bear to hear any excuses for abuse. When I step toward the basement Barry adds, "Don't even think about bothering him. He's being punished."

I skulk downstairs, wondering how to mind Barry and check in on Dennis at the same time, and decide to pay him the quickest visit possible. I gently knock on Dennis's door, but he doesn't answer, most likely because nobody likes to be seen crying. I open the door an inch and whisper into the slit, "I'm sorry. I should have listened to you." Dennis doesn't respond.

I open the door a little more and nearly fall backward when I see his face.

Dennis's right eye has already turned shades of black and blue. A purple welt on his cheek appears ready to explode. His upper lip is cracked and encrusted with blood. He looks desperate for care, but I'm not sure how to extend him any. Hugs go far in rectifying some problems, but I don't know Dennis well enough to hug him, so I sit down on his bed close enough for our knees to touch. I watch for his reaction, to see if he's too upset with me to have me this close, but his watery eyes remain focused on the TV. I follow them to a menu screen for *Leatherface: The Texas Chainsaw Massacre III*. Before long, he presses a remote control button that starts the movie.

After a slow forming New Line Cinema logo, a narrator tells of hapless victims who once fell prey to a cannibalistic clan of serial killers. When the narration concludes, a sledgehammer rises. A woman's screaming face fills the screen. The sledgehammer swings forward. A vicious white splat forms the title. Between credits, a filthy, hulking man slaps down the woman's severed face onto a workbench, cuts the skin into pieces, and stitches them back together. Dennis leans forward with a grin, as though death has fulfilled him.

"Why does this make you happy?" I ask.

He replies, "Because I'm not her."

Someone in the hallway clears his throat. Fearing Barry's arrival, I bounce away from Dennis and look to Nathan with mild relief. He's standing in the door frame with his lips curled over his teeth and his eyes sunken in a gloomy haze. "Come upstairs," he says to me, "we need to talk."

I follow Nathan upstairs, which takes quite awhile since he can only manage one slow step at a time. In the living room, a wooden chair is already set before his recliner. Two full glasses of lemonade are waiting on the end table. When I sit down, Nathan eases into his recliner and hands me a sweaty glass. I haven't had a drink since biking through the sun, and I suck down half before realizing I must look like an animal. Nathan waits for my final swallow before saying, "We're not bad people."

"No, sir," I reply.

"We just need to make sure you keep a low profile."

"I understand, but I'm not used to hiding."

He rotates his wedding band a full three-hundred-and-sixty degrees, releasing a steady stream of breath. "About this morning."

"You don't have to explain."

"Aside from Lori, who's not much of a personality, there hasn't been a female presence in this house since my wife had a stroke two months ago." He leans to his left and pries out a wallet from his right pants pocket. He opens it, sorts through a plastic accordion, and extracts a small picture that he hands to me. On a park bench, seated beside an impossibly young Nathan, is a youthful woman with light hair and dark glasses. Their hands are entwined and they're smiling.

"Come this September, Gail and I will have been married fifty-four years." The baby monitor on the TV stand crackles. A moan sounds within the white noise. "You'd have liked her. She once had an association with God. When she was in her late teens she was in practice to become a nun, but then she met a certain churchgoer." He softly puts a hand on his chest. "We courted quietly for several months, and were on the verge of calling it quits so she could continue with her vows but . . . you see, she became pregnant."

"With Barry?"

"No. With a child who didn't survive the repercussions." He motions to continue, but pauses and looks away from me. "You might be too young for this."

"Not anymore."

He focuses on my eyes, as if trying to survey the damage the past several days have caused me, and decides to continue. "Gail was too afraid to tell her Mother Superior, so she trusted the help of a priest whom she thought would protect her. Instead, he took their conversation to the roof of her convent and shoved her over the edge. She hit concrete, shattered her skull, cracked her spine, and crushed the baby. She's been nearly blind and has limped ever since."

"That priest was defrocked and imprisoned, I hope."

"He's still active. She tried turning him in, but he said she had attempted suicide. Case closed." Nathan stares angrily off and grinds his false teeth. "The church has ways of protecting their own."

"Not all priests cause harm, for what it's worth."

"In any event, last night I felt a bit of warmth return to this house, and I followed it downstairs to the source." He places his hands in his lap while his bottom lip quivers. "My apologies. It's a lapse I won't make again."

I return his photograph and say, "I'm flattered you thought of me in such a way, but I've already forgiven you." He exhales through tight lips. When a tear escapes from his left eye, I decide it's best to move on to a new subject. "What time should I be ready tomorrow?"

"For?"

"Church. I need someone to take me, but I don't know what time anyone gets up on Sundays."

"Do you think it's wise to go?"

"Any church will do. Please. I need it now more than ever."

"What time do you normally attend?"

"Eight."

"Make it nine and we have a deal. Barry will be waiting." He winks at me and leans close to say in a hushed tone, "Go back to Dennis. There's no need for him to suffer because my son went off the deep end."

"Thank you for understanding, sir."

Nathan nods with a proud huff and waves me away.

I finish my drink, put the glass on the end table, and head downstairs to Dennis. On the way past Jeremy's room, I hear a movie playing that can only be one we just rented, which means Dennis will be free to go outside without him. I turn into his room, where he's sitting on his bed and holding a wet rag to his cheek. His eyes remain fixed on the TV, even when I sit beside him and say, "You're not punished anymore. Want to go out back and do something?"

"The asshole watching our movies will follow," he replies. "If I see him, I'll murder him."

"We could be quiet."

He moves the rag to his split lip, hisses through clenched teeth, and slaps the bed in three hard successions. He clearly needs time alone, at least until his pain subsides, so I oblige him. Determined to breathe fresh air, I put on my new bikini, tiptoe past Jeremy's room, grab a large towel from the bathroom, and head upstairs. Nathan is half-reclining in his chair, his eyes closed. I tell him I'm going to the pool, but he responds with a sentence from a dream that makes no sense to me.

Outside in the still-ascending heat, I dunk my feet in the foot bath and climb up a three-step ladder to the pool deck. I touch my toes to the cold water, sit on my towel with my feet emerged, and watch a leaf glide across the surface. When I tilt my head toward the sky to absorb the sun, the back door opens. I whisper a prayer that it isn't Jeremy, and open my eyes to find Dennis approaching. I cover my bare stomach with a loose part of the towel when Dennis rests his arms on the pool's frame. "So anyway," he says, "what did you think of the video store?"

"Impressive," I reply.

"Sorry I made you stay in the one section."

"I don't mind. I'm actually curious as to why you like those movies. I thought they were made for budding psychotics."

"They're therapeutic. They kill people so I don't have to." He starts bouncing awkwardly, as though he has to go to the bathroom, but he's actually taking off his sneakers and socks without using his hands. After dunking his feet in the bath, he climbs up and sits beside me. He looks at the sun, squeezes his eyes tight, and without warning pulls off his shirt. When he leans back to toss it near the bench, his smooth stomach dips under the curve of his rib cage. I've only seen shirtless men during locker room interviews on ESPN, but with no fourth wall barricading Dennis's naked torso, I feel a tickling twitch in my belly that's much more soothing than the constant wrenching of recent days. I put my crucifix charm in my mouth and kick my feet in and out of the water, but neither action can diffuse the quivers in my stomach.

"Jesus doesn't mind when you eat Him?" Dennis asks. I let the crucifix drop from my mouth, but can't keep my legs from kicking. As much as I love Sister Alice for her three years of raising me, she omitted a few necessities in preparing me for the real world, such as adolescent aches over pool dress. "Can you swim?"

"Probably not," I reply.

"Everyone's got to learn some time." He slides into the water and tenses at the cold. He bounces around the pool's circumference, to avoid a small mass of dirt in the middle, and stops before the ladder when returning to me. "Just ease yourself in and don't panic. Remember, you're taller than the water."

As I stand up to climb down the ladder, Nathan walks out back with a cordless phone. He holds it out to me and says, "It's for you."

Who else would call me but Sister Alice?

"Save my place," I say to Dennis, and hurry to Nathan for the phone. The excitement I feel from potentially swimming switches gears to a more familiar source as I grab the phone. "Hello?"

"Robin," Sister Alice says with relief. "I got worried when I didn't hear from you."

"I'm sorry. Your phone's been busy and things got hectic. How are you holding up?"

"As well as I can. A few days ago you kids were running circles around me. Now the house is so . . . empty."

"Any word on when we can come home?"

"Not yet, I'm afraid."

"I'll keep praying my hardest."

"You and me both." A sudden wind lashes through the mouthpiece. "Are you outside? Did I catch you at a bad time?"

I walk around to the side of the house so Dennis

can't hear me. "I'm near the pool and just saw a boy half naked and my stomach went crazy. Does that count as lust? If it does, I'm in big trouble."

Sister Alice laughs emphatically. "You're growing up, sweetheart. You'll be attracted to boys, and boys will be attracted to you. As long as you don't physically act on your desires, you'll be fine."

"Okay, good. Because I don't want to miss out on swimming to make penance."

"Then don't let me stop you. Go on and have fun."

"No-no-no! That's not what I meant! I want to talk to you!"

"Call me afterward, okay? Enjoy your stay."

"Okay. I promise I'll call you right after."

"Deal." We make kisses and hang up.

I eagerly turn from the side of the house to a scene that destroys every ounce of my delight. Jeremy is standing atop the pool deck with his private parts pulled from his shorts. "Either vacuum that shit up," he says, "or I'll hose your ass down."

Dennis, still in the water, scrambles as far away as he can and says, "It's your turn, dickhead!"

Jeremy lets loose an arched stream of urine that sends Dennis hopping over the side of the pool as though he's avoiding a live grenade. I sneak back into the house and attempt to call Sister Alice, but am again greeted by the answering machine. I feel awful for not speaking to her when I finally had the chance, and prepare to face an afternoon of staring at walls as punishment.

About an hour after dinner—the saltiest Chinese food I've ever eaten—Dennis comes into my room with a look of complete despair. His face is so pale the bruises stand out tenfold.

"What's wrong?" I ask.

Dennis wrinkles up his nose. "Because I showed you around town, my turn to feed the old lady has been bumped up. I could use some support, if you don't mind." Curious as to why the task seems so daunting, and eager to meet the woman Nathan told me about, I agree to help him.

I follow Dennis to a green-carpeted stairwell leading to the second floor. Along the way we pass framed photographs of presumed family members. One displays Barry and Lori touching champagne glasses during their wedding ceremony. Lori looks happy and Barry is nearly thin.

When I step onto the landing upstairs, I hear the sounds of a baseball game through a closed door. The home crowd is in an uproar. I want to peek in to see what's happening, but suddenly recall Barry's allegiance to the Yankees, and focus on an alternate sound. Across the hall, behind another closed door, Lori's faint voice can be heard as though she's reading aloud.

Dennis continues down a dark hallway toward a room with a half-open door. Before venturing inside, he takes a deep breath. The dread in his eyes makes me take a deep breath too.

The bedroom we enter is certainly out of the ordinary, but hardly a call for concern. Common furnishings are in short supply, since the space has been altered into an orderly hospital room. On an adjustable bed lies an elderly woman wearing a white cotton nightgown. A white sheet covers her from the hips down. Her head is turned sideways and her face is buried beneath long, stringy white hair. A metal stand beside her holds an assortment of vials and pills, but a running air conditioner sucks out their medicinal scents. A baby monitor sits on the night stand.

Dennis opens a dresser drawer and extracts a red plastic pouch and two jars of baby food; mango and pear. He uncaps the jars and shakes their contents into the pouch. I hold the crossbar at the foot of the bed while observing the woman Nathan said had a stroke. "Does she ever come around?" I ask.

"Enough so they can keep her here," Dennis replies, "but she rarely makes sense when she is awake. She thinks I'm the train conductor who took her to Peoria when she was four."

Dennis scrapes the baby food jars empty with a plastic spoon, screws a perforated tube into the bag's opening, and retracts a jar of lubricant from the drawer. After smearing two fingers worth of clear jelly onto the hose, he props Gail upright on her pillow so she's facing forward. Her hair remains over her face. Dennis parts the mass over her mouth and separates her jaws by pressing against her molars. As he slides the tube steadily into her mouth, I make sure to remain still so I don't cause him to slip. When satisfied with the injected length of hose, Dennis begins squeezing the pouch, which sends baby food streaming through the piping and straight down the old woman's throat.

"Do you think she's suffering?" I whisper.

"Probably," he whispers back. "It's not like you're allowed to be happy around here. Which is why I wanted to ask you about church."

The bed starts to shudder as Gail's legs suddenly shake. When her foot kicks the crossbar I jump back with a scream. Gail's hands thrash about as she feels the bed sheets, her nightgown, and eventually the lodged tube. She tries pulling it out, but is biting down at the same time. Dennis attempts to separate her clamped jaws and says in a panic, "Gail, relax! I'll get it out!"

The floor rumbles. Barry barges inside. He rushes past me, shoves Dennis into a wall, and yanks the tubing free from Gail's throat. Baby food, lubricant, and saliva fly in all directions. Barry smacks Dennis across the face with the dripping tube and yells, "Can't you do anything right? This poor girl must think you're an asshole!"

Rather than defend himself, Dennis hurries away. Barry looks at me and tries to fake a smile, but he's too frenzied to pull one off. He turns to Gail and pets her forehead. When she eases back into stillness, I slip out of the room and head downstairs.

Dennis is sitting at the edge of his bed and rubbing his hands together. A vein in his temple throbs. "I hate that pig so much," he growls.

Rather than address why it's wrong to put hate into any living creature, I go a route that will alleviate his pain faster. Looking over his movies I ask, "Do any of these have an obese man in peril?"

"I'm not finding any positives in this dump." He looks at me with soft, wet eyes. "Religion seems to keep you going. Would you mind if I go to church with you tomorrow?"

Happiness flows through my head and heart so

fast I dizzily drop down into his computer chair. I've always been eager to share my religious experiences with someone my own age, and have gotten too used to keeping quiet about my beliefs because nobody ever wants to hear about them. That Dennis takes an interest makes me want to hug him until his eyes bulge, but I'm still not sure if I should make physical contact with him, so I simply say, "I'd love your company."

He smiles with contentment and then heads for the hallway.

"Where are you going?"

"Jeremy will be out for a while. I'm getting *C.H.U.D.* back." When Dennis leaves I feel my butterflies whirling with satisfaction. I bounce my legs up and down, then cover my face in case he comes back and sees how red I must be turning.

Dennis and I sit on his bed, our backs against the headboard, with a bowl of microwave popcorn between us. He loads the film in a gloomy state, but when *C.H.U.D.*'s title appears after a woman is yanked into a sewer by a monstrous hand, his rigid posture slackens and cheer fills his eyes. Death has once again satisfied him, but it's the only murder within the first hour of the film. In place of gore are religious connotations I'm not sure Dennis has picked up on. The film centers on a man named Shepherd, who others refer to as Reverend. He's a cook for the homeless (referred to by a cop as a flock) who live underground and are largely forgotten by the overhead world. The homeless rave about the need for weapons to protect themselves from whatever showed its hand in the opening scene, yet nobody but the Reverend seems to care. Despite how dangerous the situation is, he'll stop at nothing to protect others.

Maybe I've been primed to see the religious side of even the most sour aspects of life, but *C.H.U.D.* strikes a chord as to why Dennis would want to seek out religion. On the surface it might seem obvious, that those who live underground long for a savior, and if such is the case I'm more than happy to provide a shot at salvation for someone so undeservedly mistreated. If one good thing can come of my staying here, I hope it's to help the most destitute member of the household.

When events in the movie start to pick up, meaning C.H.U.D.s actually appear, knuckles rap loudly on the open door. Barry is observing us with eyes primed to shoot laser beams, even though we aren't doing anything wrong. We're merely sitting back against the headboard with our hands near a shared popcorn bowl.

"I don't like this one bit," Barry exclaims. "Boy, get your ass on the floor!" Dennis slides off the foot end with a soft groan. "You'll want to watch that attitude, sport!"

Barry looks to me with a much kinder facade. "I'm thinking maybe you should wear something to church you've never worn before, like a disguise. I put a few of Lori's outfits on your bed. Why don't you go try them on?"

I get up quickly to appease Barry's mood, and so I can get back to Dennis as soon as possible. After hurrying into my room, I close the door, strip out of my pajamas, and throw on the outfit on the top of the pile of clothes; an orange sleeveless sweater and a dark green skirt. The skirt is a little tight around the hips, but I'm able to move without hindrance. The sweater fits perfectly. Satisfied, I remove the outfit.

While standing in just my bra and panties, the doorknob jiggles. I clasp my forearms over my breasts and curl my body sideways as the door swings open. Barry leans inside and says, "Let's see how they look!" He sees me and blushes, an indication he'll retreat, but instead his eyes slowly graze me from my bare feet to my concealed chest.

"Excuse me!" I say.

Barry finally blinks and backs away as awareness

creeps into his overheated face. I throw on my pajamas and meet him in the hall where he stands with his hands cupped over the naughty spot under his gut. His voice rattles when he says, "You couldn't have tried them all on."

"The first outfit will do, thank you. Is eight-thirty okay to leave?"

He tries keeping his eyes fixated on mine, but they keep descending toward other areas. His complexion never lightens from its dark hue. "What do you say I join you two for the rest of the movie? Looks like fun in there."

My mouth opens but I utter no words. He'll only cast an uncomfortable cloud over the rest of the evening, but I could never imply something so harsh. When his eyes widen to force a response from me, I hesitantly say, "Sounds good."

He glares at me with a corrosive smirk. "Make sure he keeps his distance. You'll never know when I'll be back down."

After Barry heaves himself upstairs, Dennis reclaims his position on the bed and pats my spot. As much as I don't want to disregard Barry's authority, I want Dennis to know he has someone on his side who's willing to bend the rules in his favor. I compromise by sitting on the bed while keeping one foot planted on the floor. In always watching the doorway during loud moments, or listening for hallway sounds during quiet spots, I never regain the mild enjoyment *C.H.U.D.* had initially instilled in me.

Just past midnight, after laying in my own bed for two hours without any signs of falling asleep, I sneak outside and sit atop the pool deck. A breeze lessens the heat, but the humidity is still bonding to my skin. When my mind wanders away from the deceased children and whether or not Sister Alice is able to sleep, I find comfort in thinking about Dennis and having someone to go to church with. The church closest to this house, and the one we'll most likely attend, opened just three months ago. I've never been there, but Sister Alice is always praising its modern designs. Father Vincent Hartman, the priest my group home is named after, was recently issued control over the church and its parishioners. Though I've only seen him in passing, perhaps if I run into him he can shed some light on recent events.

When a car pulls into the driveway, I sneak to the side of the house for a look, fearing Jeremy has returned home and might decide on a midnight dip. Instead, in the light of the moon I find Nathan helping Gail out of Barry's SUV. Her nightgown and the hair that covers her face appear patched with blood. Worried they need help, I meet them inside at the front door. Nathan greets me with stunned eyes and asks, "Why aren't you in bed?"

"I don't sleep well," I reply. "Is she okay?"

"She fell out of bed and cut her head. She'll be fine."

I keep watching them, because the amount of blood on Gail is extensive. Nathan, clearly upset I won't leave, sits Gail on the steps, walks closer to me, and softly says, "I appreciate your concern, Robin, but they gave her seven stitches and the bleeding has stopped. Why scalps let out so much blood is beyond me."

Gail leans sideways against the railing with an elongated moan.

"Please don't tell anyone about this. Barry is one excuse away from putting her in a home. I can't lose her."

"I won't say anything. I promise."

Nathan kisses the top of my head and returns to his wife. He carefully leads her up the stairs one rung at a time. I watch with admiration, as we should all be so lucky to have someone with whom to grow old.

CHAPTER IV

Dennis and I head upstairs at eight-thirty on the dot, dressed for church and ready to go. Barry is standing at the kitchen counter sipping coffee. He's wearing dark blue jeans and a tight blue Polo shirt that does nothing to conceal his girth. Before he even looks at us he says with a marginal laugh, "I don't think so, buddy. Go back to bed."

Dennis leans his head all the way back and groans, "But I didn't do anything!"

Barry slams his mug down on the counter. Coffee splashes upward and onto the base of his thumb. He shrieks and sucks on the skin. Dennis, clearly unwilling to take the brunt of Barry's rage, shoots downstairs. Just like that, his company, and my anticipation of sharing my sanctuary with him, are gone.

Barry looks at me with a bright smile, plucks the front of his shirt from his breast divides, and delightfully says, "Coffee?" I shake my head. I want nothing from him but his ability to drive.

Barry puts a hand on my shoulder and leads me all the way out to his car. He lets go when I climb into the passenger seat, but as soon as he plunges into the driver's side his hand lands on my knee. I want to tell him to remove it, but am afraid he'll refuse to take me where I need to go.

Barry doesn't speak during the ride to church. He's too busy singing along to country music. His voice is enthusiastic, even though the primary singer is melancholy. He taps on my thigh to drum beats, strums his fingers on my forearm to guitar leads, and twiddles his fingers against my neck to chorus lyrics. When his right arm isn't performing, it lies over my headrest. I have the strangest feeling he thinks we're on a date.

Arriving at church, I observe well-dressed strangers as they make their way to God's newly established house. Unlike the church I'm used to attending, which is white with peeling paint and settled on a lawn of dandelions, this one is built of dark brown wood and stands on a bed of thick green sod. None of the sidewalk grids on the way to the front door have weeds, and the stoop is free of cracks and moss. The inside is much cleaner as well. The tops of the pew backings are still glossy and don't display the black sludge from grip wear, the stained glass windows are vibrant, and

the polished floor squeaks under my shoes. The crucifix behind the altar, though distant, is much more
realistic than any I've ever seen. Jesus's pained eyes
appear wet and blood seems to drip from his wounds.

Barry follows me into a pew three rows from the
entrance. Nobody around us seems concerned with
a newcomer, which is a blessing since I don't need
the attention, but I do feel a bit awkward attending
my first mass outside my usual surroundings. That
discomfort wavers when mass begins with Father
Vincent walking down the aisle swinging an urn of
incense. Seeing a somewhat-familiar face sets me at
ease.

Father Vincent proves he's a worthy alternative to
the priest I'm accustomed to. Despite his advanced
age, he speaks loudly, has a strong singing voice, and
displays an enthusiasm that clears the languidness
from most everyone's eyes. Most importantly, he never seems weary of what he's preaching.

Barry maintains his composure throughout the
mass, but moans to himself whenever we're instructed
to rise and sit again. He also places fingers in his ears
when the woman next to him sings loudly. He doesn't
complain verbally, but his yawns gradually become
elongated growls.

When in line for the Eucharist, which Barry understandably sits out, I feel eager to greet Father Vincent face to face. I hope he'll be happy to see someone from his group home still practicing the sacraments despite the recent crimes. As he puts the body of Christ in my mouth, however, he looks at me blankly before eyeing the next patron.

When mass ends, Barry springs upright and motions for me to get moving by waving his arms toward the aisle. "May I have a minute with the priest?" I ask.

His shoulders slump and he huffs, "That wasn't part of the deal."

"I know, but I need to speak with him and don't want to have to ask for another ride."

"How long will it take? Breakfast has been knocking on my back door since the first psalm."

"Just one minute."

"Fine. You have a minute. I'll be in the car."

When Barry leaves, I wait in the pew as Father Vincent greets those who wish to speak to him at the front door. After shaking hands with the last person, he heads down the aisle and passes me without noticing my eyes on him. While removing his stole, he stops short and suspiciously looks back. Our eyes meet and I offer him a smile. He cocks his head and says, "Have we met?"

"I'm Robin," I reply. He squints and looks upward, as though God will remind him who I am. "Robin Hills?"

"Of course! Robin who lives with Alice." He approaches me while folding his garment. I scoot over to give him room beside me. He sits close enough that I can smell his breath, which reeks of fruity ammonia. "How are you holding up?"

"I'm not sure. I've been having thoughts of God I've never had before."

"Given the circumstances, I'm not surprised."

"Have you ever wondered if He turned His back on us?"

"I used to, when I was your age. The state of the world would make me wonder if anyone was up there at all. But then I'd ask myself how much worse we'd all be if He wasn't. Chaos would be everywhere, wouldn't it? You and I wouldn't be able to sit here without someone kicking down the door and taking out their aggression on us."

"But why do the innocent have to pay the price for the ones who deny God? Why do we have to enjoy every day like it's our last because their souls are empty?"

"Maybe God puts them here to make us enjoy life more."

"That doesn't seem fair."

"My best advice is to stay close to those who make life worthwhile. They're out there. I wouldn't have remained a priest if I didn't believe the good outweighed the bad." Father Vincent's hands are shaking beneath his stole. He catches me gazing at them, stands from the pew, and rubs his palms together. "If you'll excuse me, Robin, I have another mass to prepare for."

"Of course, Father. Thank you for your time." He smiles with a nod and walks away while erratically arching his neck.

Before leaving, I light four votive candles at a shrine of the Virgin Mary; one for the children in God's kingdom, one for the safety of the survivors, one for Sister Alice to ensure she'll get by on her own, and one for Dennis to improve his miserable family life.

When we get home, Barry hobbles inside and hurries upstairs. I plan to call Sister Alice and tell her about the new church she's been raving about, but am met with an unexpected visitor.

Detective Morris, head of the murder investigations, is sitting on the couch with a full glass of lemonade in hand. His eyes are dark and dour. I hope he's come to check on me, and not to spread bad news, but Nathan stands from his chair and heads straight for the stairs without bothering to look at me. When alone with Detective Morris I say, "I don't want to know."

"Please," he replies, "sit down." I sit on the very edge of Nathan's chair, close enough to the detective to smell that he hasn't washed his suit jacket in a while. He also looks as though he hasn't slept in weeks. His eyes are bloodshot, his hair is unkempt, while his skin is slick and pimply. After running his hands over his face he finally begins: "The rectory Father Vincent resides in was broken into last night. We tried keeping your locations confidential, but he admits maintaining handwritten records. They were stolen."

"Someone knows where we are?"

"I'm afraid so."

"Does this mean I'm leaving?"

He twirls his hands as though searching for words and blurts out, "Another child was killed last night. Peter Heffernan."

I grab the armrests for support as the room immediately spins. I open my mouth to ask how, or why such an atrocity could occur under the watch of the law, but instead have to stifle a scream. Peter came to us only three months ago, but I quickly became attached to him. Whenever I'd turn my back on him he'd make himself filthy with dirt or food so he could spend time with the bath boats. Even Sister Alice had a hard time keeping up with him, and she's been taking care of kids for decades.

Detective Morris says something in a comforting tone, but I can't distinguish his words as my ears are pulsating with the beat of my heart. I somehow get to my feet and stagger to the kitchen to call Sister Alice to see how she's taking the news, if she even knows, but two hands land on my shoulders and lead me back to the chair. "First of all," Detective Morris says sternly, "I'm not going to let anything happen to you or Amanda."

"Sounds familiar."

"The best course of action would be to relocate you out of state, but we haven't a clue as to who's doing this. There are no hairs, no fibers, no prints, no leads, no nothing. All we have are the extracted eyes that link the murders. Who's to say if we move you to another home the crimes won't spread to other children? As of now, you're our best bet at catching this guy."

"As bait?"

"The houses where you're all staying have been under surveillance since the move, but obviously that hasn't been enough. I'm increasing the watch with undercover cops equipped with enough ammo to take down the devil himself. Someone will try to get to you, but I promise they won't."

"Wouldn't my staying put everyone who lives here in danger?"

"For all I know, every child on the island is in danger."

I drop back into the recliner, wondering how so much pressure can fall upon someone with so few experiences in life. Last month I was studying for sophomore finals, today I'm putting lives on the line as a means to salvage others. "Let me be the focus. Move Amanda as far away as possible."

"Ordinarily that would be a great idea, but two chances are better than one." Mr. Morris places a gentle hand on my fist, and looks upon me with impassive eyes. "God as my witness, you'll both survive." I have no choice but to accept his strict promise, as my options are limited. Running from this will potentially leave more victims in my wake.

After Detective Morris leaves, I head straight to my room and throw myself onto the bed. I need time to let everything settle before calling Sister Alice, since it's probably best to let the shock wear off before trying to speak rationally. With nobody to console me, I reach for my Bible, but for the first time since I've been introduced to its teachings I can't bring myself to open it. I've been unclear on God's intentions with His children, particularly the fallen, but have been under the assumption He salvaged some of us for a specific reason. I believed God had a hand in transferring me from a life of squalor to one of divinity. That we're still dying nullifies any significance we might have had in His divine plan. At that I feel expendable and worthless.

After about an hour of trying to calm myself, I call Sister Alice from the kitchen phone, but am met with a pulsing tone. I figure she's probably on the line with the police or others in the church who know what's happened, but after trying for close to two hours I start to worry she had an accident, tried calling for help, and is laying on the floor unable to dial. Or maybe the killer got to her too. These days it's becoming normal to suspect the worst. Unfortunately, the only way I'll know for sure is to ask Barry for help.

Upstairs, I knock heavily on a door that muffles a loud car commercial. Chair springs squeal and hefty footsteps approach. A lock unfastens with an acute gyration, and Barry opens up with bright anger that turns to pleasant surprise when he notices me. "Robin," he says, "I wasn't sure if I should . . . try to talk to you about . . . what happened to that kid. Did you want to talk about it?"

"I have a favor to ask," I say. "I was wondering if you could drive me some place."

"I don't know, sugar. Church was risky enough."

"This place wouldn't be risky. The killer already knows I've been moved from there. I haven't been able to reach Sister Alice and I'm really worried about her."

Barry bows his head, compressing his chins into one glob, and issues a wet burp that smells like vinegar and Cheetos. "Tell you what: if no more kids die between now and sundown, I'll think about it. There's no way I'm driving you in broad daylight."

"Understood. Thank you." I turn to leave, but Barry snatches my arm.

"Not so fast! I gave you an hour at church, you can give me an hour here." He pulls me into his room, unfolds an aluminum chair, and sets it beside a blue recliner whose springs scream to a halt when he sits back down. Though I try to keep my eyes away from the TV, which is airing a Yankees game, I can't block out the paraphernalia that barrage every corner of the room. The walls are filled with team photographs of World Series winning lineups, two glass-enclosed towers carry modern souvenirs and framed tickets, numerous shelves are littered with figurines and signed baseballs. Not even the ceiling is safe, as a large canvas banner with the Yankees logo is sprawled above us. I have no choice but to watch the game, since that area at least provides movement and the possibility of a loss. The Yankees, however, are already beating the Angels by three runs in the second inning.

I take a seat with a polite smile, figuring an hour of Yankees baseball won't kill me as long as I root for the other team. Doing so, nevertheless, proves incredibly difficult. Whenever an Angel makes an out, Barry claps or laughs like a demented clown. He also squawks and pumps his fist every time a Yankee gets a hit. All I can do is pray the Angels will spark a rally to put Barry in his place, but the Yankees take an early 8-2 lead.

When I'm freed to go, I dial the group home from the kitchen and yet again am met with a busy signal. Hoping to spend time with Dennis I head to the basement, but he's in Jeremy's room. Jeremy is berating him with swear words I can barely comprehend. When he catches me gazing at him from the open door he says, "Listen to me carefully, Jesus fucker. I just heard on the news that another little shit from your house was vaporized, so keep your God fearing ass away from me! I like my eyes exactly where they are!" He slams the door in my face. Attached at eye level is a handwritten sign that reads, *INNOCENT BYSTANDER, ZEALOT DOWN THE HALL!*

I turn in disgust, only to find my bedroom door marred with further insensitivities. Written in bold letters on attached construction paper is, *THE ORPHAN'S IN HERE!* I tear it off, rip it in half, kick the door shut, and sit on the bed while wringing my hands. The patience I was taught to display through high and low is dissolving. My butterflies are drowning in bile, and I have no means of saving them. If I don't get to see Sister Alice tonight, I might explode.

At around eight o'clock, Barry opens my door without knocking. Though hc sees I'm laying on my bed staring at the ceiling he asks, "What are you up to?"

"This," I reply.

"How would you like to . . ." he prolongs the last vowel to build suspense, but his avid eyes give up his scheme.

"I'd love to visit her!"

Barry belches into his fist and pats his lower stomach. "Give me five minutes. I think those potato wedges were cooked in motor oil." When he hobbles away I jump up and think of how great it would be to bring Dennis along, especially since he missed out on church.

I stand at Dennis's door, building up the courage to enter, since Jeremy is hollering obscenities and won't be thrilled when I interrupt whatever movie they're watching. I creep inside, dimly hoping Jeremy won't notice me, and whisper to Dennis, "Would you like to visit Sister Alice with me? We're leaving soon."

Jeremy cracks a laugh and says, "Why would he want to visit that hag? Some whore is about to take a fishing gaff through her twat. Too bad she looks nothing like you."

Dennis shuts off the movie and reaches for his sneakers. Jeremy hocks up about ten pounds of snot and spits a wad onto the TV screen. It sticks without running. I step aside as he rushes into the hallway muttering something about how sorry we'll both be.

Dennis and I sit on the living room couch while waiting for Barry to come down. A toilet above us keeps flushing, and a tank lid keeps clanking. Instead of envisioning the cause, I half-observe a TV special about Korean War tanks that Nathan is watching, even though his eyelids are begging for sleep. Dennis leans into me and says, "If you ask him about his role in that war he'll be your best friend forever."

"Seriously?" I reply.

Dennis nods, so I say quite loudly to Nathan, "What did you do in Korea?"

Nathan's eyes snap open. He shifts upright in his chair, puts a hand over his heart, and says with beaming pride, "Bomb technician! I built the explosives that destroyed dozens of Zips at a time. Mortars, land mines, delay action time bombs, you name it." He looks back at the TV with a contented smile. "Those sure were the days."

I can't justify why Nathan is so happy to have had a hand in killing by the dozens, but do take comfort that he is happy in remembering his youth. As I mull over a way to continue, Barry hops downstairs while whistling a merry tune. When seeing Dennis, he plunks to a stop and says, "You don't give up, do you?"

Dennis replies, "I thought I could go with her and—"

"And nothing! Back downstairs in three . . . two . . ."

"For crying out loud," Nathan says, "she wants him to meet her nun."

"Butt out, Dad! He deserves to be punished!"

"He's been punished enough! Let him go."

Barry tears open the front door, storms outside, and unleashes one of the loudest F-bombs I've ever heard. Dennis and I tentatively approach his car, where Barry gets inside so fast the driver's side shocks grind to a halt before bouncing back up. When the passenger doors unlock, Dennis is quick to take the backseat, which makes sense, as Barry has never taken out his anger on me.

As soon as I close the front passenger door and start fastening my seat belt, Barry backs out of the driveway with too much emphasis on the gas pedal and brakes. While he jerks us about and fills the car with steamy tension, my butterflies flutter in nervous anticipation of whether or not I'll find Sister Alice safe and sound.

Barry drives to the group home high above the speed limit and doesn't brake for red lights or stop signs until a few feet away from them. Dennis sits pressed to the backseat with his eyes fused. While closing in on my old block, Barry says, "You need to get out right away. He shouldn't see you in my car, in case he's watching. I'll park down the street."

"Sounds like a plan," I say.

"Don't *plan* on staying all night." When he rolls up to the house beside the group home, Dennis and I leap out onto the street without any time to close our doors. Barry speeds away so fast they shut by themselves.

I take Dennis by the shirt sleeve, run with him to the group home, and ring the doorbell in three quick successions. I hear Sister Alice's slippers shuffling to the door, a reassuring sign she's alive, where she presumably checks the peep hole before opening up with a beaming smile. She extends her arms to me and says, "Robin!" I hug her a lot harder than I probably should, but stop the moment she presses me away. "Easy, sweetheart, I'm no spring chicken!"

"Sorry, it's just that . . . I'm just so glad to see you!"

"I know how you feel. Who's your friend?"

Dennis extends his hand to her. "I'm Dennis. Nice to meet you, ma'am."

Sister Alice gently accepts his hand into both of hers. "You're taking care of my little girl, I hope?"

"She's pretty capable of taking care of herself, but I've been keeping her company."

"Glad to hear. Come sit down." She takes my hand and leads me to the couch where I ease in close beside her. Dennis sits in an adjacent recliner. I try to breathe in the familiar scents, but they're overshadowed by four candles burning on the coffee table. Three are nearing their end, one is fresh. I know they're for the fallen, but don't say so. I need time to catch up with the living.

On TV, the Mets are down by one run to the Pirates. "Have they won since I left?" I ask.

"They've been getting creamed, but managed to score a run just now." When she smiles, the lines in her face crinkle more than they used to. Her eyes are dry and worn. She looks to have aged ten years in the short time I've been away. I wriggle myself closer to her and rest my head on her shoulder.

"Do you know how much I miss your voice?"

"As a matter of fact, I do. It's been unusually quiet around here."

"It's weird not seeing toys all over the rug."

"It's weirder that I miss tripping over them."

"We'll be back together soon. Despite everything, I'm still praying."

"True to your word." She adjusts herself to face Dennis, who sits up attentively. "She's been devout since the day I took her in, you know." I recoil, and probably blush, because I know she's about to tell a story I often hear in front of people I've just met. "When Robin arrived here I told her the story of Job, to coincide with the difficulty of her upbringing. Are you familiar with him?"

"He's the guy God torments to test his faith," Dennis says.

"You should also know, then, that God's reward

was giving Job twice what He'd taken away. When I finished telling Robin the story, she looked at me with the most bemused eyes and said, 'So if I believe in God, He'll return two childhoods?' Let me tell you, my heart just melted."

Dennis eases back into the chair with, "She's prone to do that."

Sister Alice looks at me with a pleased hum. I pretend not to have heard him, and focus on the game. That Dennis is kind to me is one thing, but that he thinks of me in such a tender way isn't something I anticipated. Having no idea how to handle the matter, I decide to change the subject and say, "Can I ask you something kind of gloomy?"

"If it's about the Mets," Sister Alice replies, "talk to their batting coach."

"Are you scared to stay here?"

"Mostly at night, but the Lord will see fit to save me if that's my fate. Besides, Father Vincent decided I should remain here to show a brave face, which, I agree, is important." She lets out a distressed sigh and faces the TV, where the Mets are in trouble. Two opposing Pirates are on the corners with nobody out. The Pirates batter hits a shallow pop up. The Mets center fielder calls for the ball while running in, but stops short and lets it drop at his feet. A run scores.

Sister Alice punches the air. "For the love of Saint Augustine! Where was the charge?"

Dennis looks away with discomfort, but he needn't worry. Angst is a lesser part of Sister Alice's demeanor, and it's only brought on by the Mets. "For what they're paying him," I say, "he should have an operation to get the lead out of his butt." Sister Alice holds out a flat hand. I gently slap it five. Dennis smiles at us and we all share a subdued laugh, until a honking horn outside shatters the moment. Through the bay window I see Barry's SUV across the street. Not staying all night apparently means two measly minutes to him.

"Is that your ride?" Sister Alice asks.

"Unfortunately," I reply.

"Ah, well. Better to see you for a minute than not at all."

"We'll come back soon. I promise." I give Sister Alice a soft hug and kiss her on the cheek. She pats my back, but remains seated when I stand. She doesn't appear to have the strength left to walk us to the door, which makes me feel worse for having to leave her. Outside, Barry leans on the horn, destroying the very secrecy he himself demanded.

As soon as Dennis and I sit inside the car, Barry pulls away fast enough to make the tires squeal.

I slump forward and rest my forehead on my palms. "Some visit," Barry says, "I thought she makes you happy."

"I don't like that she's alone," I reply. Barry pats my knee, as though doing so will comfort me.

After we arrive at the house, Dennis and Jeremy finish watching whatever movie I'd interrupted, so I sneak outside to the pool and sit with my bare feet in the water. Alone in the dark, and wary of a noiseless prowler, I keep splashes to a minimum and silently pray that Sister Alice isn't going to cave under this calamity.

A little while later, the back door opens. Dennis peeks his head out. I whistle lightly to catch his attention. He climbs up the ladder, removes his flip flops, and sits beside me with his feet submerged. "How was the movie?" I ask.

"Gory," he replies, and kicks at a leaf the same time I do. Our slippery feet rub together. My butterflies flutter up from their gloomy depths, but my mind is still fixated on dismal subjects.

"If I ask you something stupid, will you be honest with me?"

"If you want."

"If I were trapped in a horror movie, would I survive?"

"Without a doubt. Survivors can usually handle the stress of losing their friends, so you've got that going for you. You'd actually be perfect in my favorite movie."

"Which one is that?"

"*Dawn of the Dead*. The original, from '78." He adjusts himself so that he faces me while his feet remain in the pool. The moonlight accentuates the sparkle in his zealous eyes. "Four people escape from a city that's overrun by zombies and hole up in a shopping mall. Once they barricade the zombies out, they have everything they could ever want. Clothes, electronics, food. I mean, they live in a mall! But there's a catch."

"The zombies get back in?"

"Which isn't their fault. They live like royalty until renegade bikers show up wanting a piece of the action. They're the ones who let the zombies back in and ruin paradise."

"And I remind you of . . ."

"One of the survivors is a woman. She's pregnant and moody, which isn't you, but she's not afraid to face all the bullshit the world hands her."

"I'm like that?"

"You were just sitting out here in the dark by yourself when someone is looking for you with bad intentions. You went to church, and the group home, instead of hiding and waiting for someone to come save you. What's going down is worse than any zombie invasion, because it's real, but you're still living the way you want."

"Maybe I am waiting for someone to save me." I lift my crucifix charm toward the moon and twist it until Jesus catches the light. "Maybe God will just never show."

"I guess at this point anyone would have doubts."

"I've been having them for weeks. I know God is aware that His world is full of sin, and that He's always watching out for evil. If you buy into Cain and Abel, it's just a matter of time before He exposes and punishes the killer. It could be tonight, or it could be when we're all dead. Only God knows for sure."

Out of the blue, Dennis takes hold of my left hand. My butterflies explode into my throat, but I swallow them back down. I look up to the stars and toward my Heaven, a place where people love all people, and nobody is ever teased or made to feel fear. Nobody shouts, nobody cries, and nobody has a mother who places them beneath drugs and abusive men. I tilt my head toward Dennis and see him looking at the sky too. "Do you have a Heaven?" I ask.

"The Monroeville Mall, where *Dawn* was filmed." He grins peacefully. "It's a real place in Pennsylvania you don't have to die to get into." I look into his eyes to try to gauge his feelings, since I have no image of his promised land. Just as he looks at me, something splashes in the pool. We cringe with fright and let go of each other to stand. My eyes take a moment to adjust before detecting a black box with a curvy tail sinking in the water.

"My DVD player!" Dennis says. "Jeremy, you fuck!"

I can't see Jeremy, but hear him say from a distance, "This is what happens when you pick the holy whore over me. Don't think I forgot!" The back door slams shut, cutting out his sinister laughter.

Dennis takes off his shirt and jumps in after his machine. He retrieves and brings it to the deck, where I immediately wrap it with my towel. "I swear to God, I'm going to kill that pile of shit!"

"Swearing won't help," I say. "Neither will killing him."

"What else can I do? Destroy his stuff? Everything he owns is already broken!"

"There are ways to punish him without resorting to violence."

"Time out doesn't work for him, Robin! He needs his ass kicked!" He lifts the DVD/VCR combo and dumps out water through the cooling vent, then tosses it onto the lawn where it crashes with a metallic twang. "Forget it. I finally found one with premium sound that doesn't eat tapes, and this is the thanks I get." He sits hard on the bench and runs his hands through his hair with a frustrated growl. I try to think of something that could get our moods back to where they were thirty-seconds ago, but I come up with nothing and sit beside him while reclaiming his hand. "I'm sorry," he says, "I didn't mean to yell at you."

"You were provoked. What I don't understand is why Jeremy gets away with so much when you clearly don't."

"I'm as surprised as you are. Barry hadn't laid a finger on me in the four years I've been here. I think he's trying to impress you."

"It's not working."

He looks at me with adoration. "We'd better go inside before Jeremy destroys the rest of my room."

I follow Dennis down to the basement, where I'm thankful for the sounds of heavy metal, as it means Jeremy is too preoccupied to bother us. I peek inside my room, pleased to see no damage or destruction, but what I find in Dennis's room is another story. Movies are thrown off the shelves, posters are torn from the walls, and a giant bowl of cereal has been splashed across the bed. We clean up without saying anything to each other, and when finished we sit side-by-side on his stripped mattress. He looks in my eyes and turns red when regarding my lips. After wiping his palms on his pants he nervously says, "Would you want to watch *Dawn of the Dead* with me? It's only violent in spurts, and I'll tell you when to cover your eyes."

Delighted to partake in his Heaven, I quickly agree.

Dennis goes into his closet for his old DVD player. The flap is broken off the sliding tray, the plastic before the clock is cracked, and the top is dented as though someone stepped on it. The device powers up, though, and eventually, after a lengthy loading time, *Dawn of the Dead* begins to play.

When a helicopter carrying four survivors of a zombie outbreak hovers over the Monroeville Mall, Dennis pumps his fist, even though his paradise is something of an eyesore. The brick exterior is as cold as the surrounding gray sky, while the empty parking lot is littered with the living dead. Yet I feel Dennis's breath softening, and ease myself into his tranquility. I can tell he's no longer thinking about his family, and I manage to put aside the danger that looms over me. In a pure state of comfort, I crawl under Dennis's arm and rest my head on his shoulder.

* * *

When back in my room, sleep doesn't come easily yet again, this time because of a thunderstorm that steadily worsens. What began as distant rumbling and sporadic flashing has turned to vibrating bangs and extended electric glowing. I can handle the storm on my own, but I'm not sure about my roommate, Amanda, wherever she may be. I keep thinking about how frightened and alone she must feel right now. On nights such as these, she'd crawl into bed beside me, always with her Kermit the Frog doll, and we'd soothe one another with each other's company. To-night I use my pillow as a poor substitute, and just as I settle back down, lightning flashes and presents a dark silhouette against the wall I'm facing.

I roll over to look outside, but see nothing but darkness. Lightning blares again, highlighting a nun squatting before my window with her hands covering her brow to peer inside. When I throw off the sheets and jump out of bed, the figure scampers toward the backyard.

I rush into Dennis's room and shake him awake. At first he fights off my hands, but when he becomes conscious he worriedly asks, "What's wrong?"

"There's someone outside my window," I reply. "A nun. Or someone dressed like a nun. There's no way it's Sister Alice, right? You saw how fragile she looked, and she only wears her habit for church. Will you come upstairs with me while I call the police?"

Less than a minute after I call 911 and tell them who I am and what I just saw, a banging sounds on the front door. I open up to a man in jeans, a white T-shirt, and a red baseball cap. He enters holding a handgun and a walkie-talkie. A police badge dangles from his right pants pocket. He moves me away from the door and asks, "Which side is your bedroom on?" I point left. He presses a button on his radio and says into the mouthpiece, "West side of the house. Over."

A voice from his device replies, "Copy that. Over."

Barry staggers downstairs while tying his bathrobe belt and says in a haze, "What happened here?"

"We received a call about a prowler," the cop replies. "An officer is scouting the yard."

Barry stands next to me, swaying, and puts his hand on my back. I allow him because he's off balance, but once his hand begins rubbing circles I slink out of his reach and sit on the couch. Dennis sits beside me.

The cop's radio crackles before an out-of-breath voice says, "I'm not finding anyone on either side. I'll check the other yards. Over."

"Cover the backs, I'll get the fronts," the cop replies, then looks directly at me with, "Don't worry about a thing. Just stay inside." He rushes outside and vanishes into the storm.

Barry closes the door, yawns widely, and asks, "What did you see?"

I don't want him to get involved with anything that could make us bond, and it is quite possible I've started seeing things, so I reply, "I don't really know. Everything has me on edge."

He points at Dennis and says, fully alert, "Stop showing her your weirdo movies! You've got the poor thing rattled!"

Lori yells down from upstairs, "Would you all shut up? Some of us have to leave for work in a few hours!"

Barry pumps two middle fingers at the ceiling, then lifts a chain to fasten the door latch when it suddenly bangs opens. I jump to my feet, preparing to flee, and pull Dennis up with me. He grabs me back so tightly his fingernails dent my skin. For the first time, however, I'm relieved to see Jeremy. He stumbles inside, soaked with rain, and confusedly looks at us with bloodshot and glassy eyes.

"Where the hell have you been?" Barry asks.

"Cool your jets, tubs," Jeremy replies. "Someone a lot drunker than me gave me a ride." Jeremy staggers past us, reeking of a sweet yet pungent aroma, and stumbles downstairs.

Barry fastens the lock, moseys to his father's chair, and plops down with an agitated huff. "I'll wait here in case the cops need me," he says, then swipes a finger across my stomach with, "I'll let you stay up if you want to keep me company."

"Thanks," I reply, "but I'm really tired." I walk past him, certain he'll find a way to touch me again, but he reclines in the chair and closes his eyes.

Dennis walks me to my room and stares outside my window. Rain is falling hard, but the thunder and lightning have moved on. "At least you know you're in safe hands," he says. "They're watching you like a hawk."

"You don't have to pretend you're not afraid of what I bring to this house."

"Pretend?" He looks at me with a confused glare, and leaves with a sharp sigh. I sit on my bed with my hands over my eyes, certain I screwed up a good thing by shunning his sincerity, but Dennis promptly returns with his pillow and a rolled-up sleeping bag. While untying the straps he says, "Whoever wants to get to you will have to trip over me."

I long to leap up and hug him, but instead take two of his fingers and gently shake his arm while saying, "Thank you." I switch my pillow to the foot end of the bed so I can sleep as close to him as possible.

CHAPTER V

In the morning, exhausted from lousy sleep and parched with thirst, I tread upstairs for a glass of orange juice. I almost back out of the kitchen when I see Lori at the counter pouring coffee into a thermos, but I press on. She speeds up her actions when she notices me, yet I still say to her, "Good morning."

Without an ounce of joy she replies, "Morning."

"Off to work?" She rolls her eyes, a clear indication she doesn't want to talk to me, but I'm curious how far she'll go in dismissing me. "May I ask what you do?"

Lori sets the thermos down with an annoyed huff, and laughs to herself before saying, "I work at a public library. I was recently requisitioned to computerize the corrupted card catalog, again, but I spend most of my day fixing the bullshit nobody around me knows how to take care of. I work on a strict deadline but nothing ever seems to get done. Happy?" I don't say anything. I look away and assume she'll leave without saying goodbye. She obviously doesn't want to like me, but I refuse to take offense because she never tries. I wonder why she agreed to let me stay in her house.

Surprisingly, she continues with, "So what's your big plan in life? Have any dreams a marriage will ruin?"

"To tell you the truth, I'm not sure I'll outlive the week."

A modest amount of concern crosses her face. I'm stunned she can emote. "You make a good point. Especially living in the basement. God starts at the bottom, doesn't he?" She picks up her thermos and leaves. Feeling neither delighted nor dispirited that she spoke to me, I fix a glass of juice and go back to my room, where Dennis is awake and staring at the ceiling with exhausted eyes.

"How did you sleep?" he asks.

"Not great," I reply. "I'm glad those cops didn't find anyone, but I couldn't keep from thinking someone was watching us. Are there curtains around here?"

"There's plenty in a closet down the hall." He stands and stretches hard, as anyone would after spending the night on a floor. "Are you up, or are you going back to bed?"

"I'm up."

"You want to do the curtains now? We just have to get tools from the garage."

"Sounds like a plan. I'll get dressed and meet you upstairs. Bring your baseball glove. I need to throw." He gives me a thumbs up and leaves for his room.

I head out back with my mitt while Dennis scrounges around in the garage for a screwdriver and matching screws. I wander to the side of the house, near my bedroom window, hoping to find evidence of the prowler, but nothing in the area suggests anyone has recently been here.

"Ten bucks says it was Jeremy," Dennis says while approaching me. "He knows how close you are to a nun."

"I realize he's deranged," I say, "but why would he go out of his way to get a habit for a five second joke?"

"He might have found one in the house. Nathan's wife was a nun for a little while. One in training, at least. Maybe she hung on to it."

"I'll add it to the ever-growing 'maybe' pile."

Dennis tosses me a baseball and puts on his glove. I put on my own and we position ourselves near the fence, relatively close to one other. At first Dennis tosses the ball so softly he might as well throw underhand. I throw back with increasing speed, letting him know I can handle the force. We gradually step farther back and throw hard enough to make the ball sizzle through the damp air. Getting rid of the ball with powerful thrusts eases my tension. When I think of the dead, I throw harder. When I think of Sister Alice, I throw even harder. When I think of the figure at my window, I throw so hard it smacks into Dennis's glove and causes him to cringe. He takes off his glove, repeatedly bends his red fingers, and gives me a nod of admiration.

"You on a team or something?" he asks.

"I use a pitch back," I reply. "They're a real pain to manage if you don't hit them directly in the middle with fastballs. Would you like me to ease up?"

"Hell, no. I can take it."

I throw several more pitches, my hardest yet, and grunt with each as I tax my body's strength. When I'm out of breath and have worked up an uncomfortable amount of sweat, I wave my throwing hand at Dennis to call him off and say, "I think I'm done. Let's hang some curtains."

On our way to my bedroom, while passing Jeremy's door, we hear something that isn't "devil music." In a voice much deeper than his shrill conversational tone, Jeremy is saying: "Oh come forth in the name of Abandon and destroy she whose name I giveth as a sign. Oh great brothers of the night—" I stare at Dennis with eyes so wide they immediately burn, especially when Jeremy shouts, "In the names of the great harlot of Babylon, and of Lilith, and of Hecate, may my lust be fulfilled! Shemhamforash! Hail Satan!"

Dennis waves me off and heads toward my room where he says, "Don't take that seriously. Ever since he bought *The Satanic Bible* he made himself the local chieftain of dark bullshit."

"What if it's not bull?" I ask. "What if he has no soul because he hawked it? What if he's channeling the killer? What if he *is* the killer?"

"He's too stupid to not have gotten caught by now, and I doubt whatever he's summoning is the cause. If your prayers go unanswered, his should too. Especially if he's bothering the Prince of Darkness before breakfast."

Comparing Jeremy's choice of religion to my own seems offensive, but I don't say so, as I'd rather not argue with Dennis. Everything I've learned about Catholicism has to do with the betterment of others, whereas Satanists, to my limited knowledge, represent the more selfish aspects of human nature, those who'd rather profit in the here and now, rather than wait for an afterlife. I also can't allow myself to process any further thoughts that Jeremy might be the killer. I could never believe God is vindictive enough to force me from a loving home and into the den of a murderer.

After hanging up a set of gray curtains, the thickest we could find, Dennis and I spend the day doing rather unspectacular things. We eat breakfast, watch a tame movie, eat lunch, and sit out by the pool. We could have gone in, but Dennis still doesn't feel comfortable swimming in what he refers to as "Jeremy's other toilet," even though he treated the water with severe amounts of chlorine. We merely sit on the deck, watching the water grow more still in the windless air. When our lack of sleep catches up to us, we agree to take naps in separate rooms.

Around seven, I'm awakened when my mattress sinks near my feet. I look up to find Nathan sitting on the end of the bed watching me with an even smile. I'm barely awake when he asks, "Do you remember what you were dreaming? You seemed at peace." I close my eyes, hoping blackness will remind me of what I last envisioned, but I see nothing. "Dreams, I find, offer all the pleasantries of life. The real world—"

Dennis stumbles through the door frame, pale and dazed.

"Best to see for yourself," Nathan somberly says. "I had Dennis put on the news for you."

I worriedly rise and walk into Dennis's room. What appears on his TV is more appalling than any movie he's shown me. Behind a female reporter are fire trucks and police cars with lights blazing. Men in black raincoats are hosing down the flaming roof of my group home. *News 12 LIVE* flares in the upper right corner.

I run upstairs, with Dennis close behind, and rip open the front door. Barry, who's just about to open it from the outer side, jumps back with angry fright. He nearly drops a bag of Chinese food that he's cradling like a newborn. He settles into a happier state when he sees it's me and says, "Hello to you too!"

"I need to get to Sister Alice," I say.

He waves a pointer back and forth while shaking his head. "It'll have to wait until after dinner. Lunch was a total bust. I sent out this kid—"

I grab him by the wrist and pull him toward his car. When he sets down the bag to keep from dropping it, I let go expecting him to keep following. He remains in place and holds his hand out to me, as though eager for another tug. "This isn't a joke, Barry! Let's go!"

I rush into the passenger seat of his SUV. Dennis

hurries into the back. I keep firm eyes on Barry, who returns a stupefied stare. Though he takes his sweet time getting into the driver's seat, his decision to follow my command keeps me from getting to the group home by bike.

Barry couldn't possibly make the drive more punishing. He never nears the speed limit, he brakes for yellow lights, he looks every direction several times at stop signs, and he whistles a slow dirge. I'd tell him the group home is on fire, but can't bring myself to say it out loud. When noting a plume of smoke above a distant tree line, his look of disinterest turns to concern and he finally reaches the speed limit.

Upon riding into my neighborhood, a burning odor sifts through the vents. Chunks of wet and dry ash land on the windshield. The wipers smear the debris into a translucent rainbow, but I can still make out a police car parked at the end of my street. An officer standing at the corner motions for us to continue moving with his switched-off flashlight. Barry pulls up beside the cop and opens his window. Vocal commotion sounds near the fire trucks and police cars. I press my hands flat on the dashboard to concentrate on breathing as my pounding heart seems to be clogging my throat.

"Keep moving, sir," the cop says. "We've got vehicles coming and going."

"Ask if there's a casualty," I say.

"Is the nun dead?" Barry asks.

"I wouldn't know," the cop replies. "I've been standing here since the medics went in."

Unable to wait on anyone for a genuine response, I jump out and race for the house. The cop yells for me to stop, but I cram myself between a thick set of hedges that lead to the backyard of a corner house and I immediately lose him. I climb over a chain link fence into another yard, and run as fast as I can until I reach a large oak tree at the side of my home. Out front, firemen are going about their duties. On the backyard grass, two police officers are having a conversation. With nobody's eyes on me, I creep to the cellar door, manage to open the combination padlock, and slip inside.

The basement is pitch black, since the windowsills are used as storage shelves and block out the light. A slim glow shines from beneath the door at the top of a six-step stairwell. Reaching out with wiggling fingers, I carefully maneuver around boxes and support poles. Once I find the railing, a noise resembling cracking knuckles sounds beneath the stairs. I look between two rungs to see if anyone is under them, but can't make out anything but a half-body mannequin in an old nun's habit.

I bolt up the steps and into the kitchen. Trails of smoke drift near the ceiling, as though the ghosts of the dead children have returned to witness the chaos. I head to the living room staircase, where I can hear the movement of heavy bodies, and their muffled voices, near Sister Alice's bedroom. The smoke up there is dense.

I hold in a deep breath, dash up the stairs, and stop short in her door frame. Every ounce of blood plummets to my feet. Atop a scorched bed lie the charred remains of Sister Alice. Her blackened limbs are contorted at odd angles. Her nightgown has disintegrated. Her skin is black where not coated with yellow and white blisters. A missing patch on her forehead exposes her skull. Her mouth is locked in a scream.

A hand lands on my shoulder and a fireman says, "You can't be in here!" Unwilling to see more, I make my way down the stairs by sliding against the wall. I head straight outside to the police and public commotion. Barry is talking to an overzealous cop who's making a lot of hand gestures. Dennis watches the house with a saddened gaze. Barry notices me approaching, blows off the cop, and opens his arms to me. I open my arms too, and walk directly into Dennis's embrace.

Dennis squeezes me tightly, kisses the top of my

head, and says, "I'm so sorry, Robin." Words can never lessen the shock, but the vibration of his voice soothes my frantic heart. I hug him back as hard as I can.

Barry storms past us saying, "We're in the way. Let's go!"

We follow him to the car, slowly, as I can't feel my legs beneath my knees. I lean on Dennis the whole way, and will probably fall over if he loosens his hold. Before climbing into the backseat with him, I look at the group home one last time, knowing I'll never have a reason to return.

When back at the house, on the way to my bedroom, Jeremy jumps out into the hall when I pass his door. He grabs me by my shoulder sleeves, pins me against the wall and says, "Looks like that psycho moved past orphans! Just because Barry and his angry bitch were stupid enough to take you in doesn't mean you get to put me in line for the slab!"

Dennis grabs him by the throat and drives him hard against the opposite wall. Jeremy swats him away and points directly at my face. "I swear to God, if that asshole plans on coming here I'll slit your fucking throat and leave you for dead on the front lawn!"

I slip into my room and shut the door. The knob briefly turns. While Dennis and Jeremy scuffle in the hallway, I slide my desk against the lock jamb.

"What the hell are you two doing?" Barry says. "She needs all the help we can give her, and you're acting like animals?"

"Like you'd be worried," Jeremy says, "it'll take forty years to burn through your fat ass!" A door bangs shut. Music starts to blare. A gentle knock sounds on my door.

"Sweetheart? It's Barry." He tries coming in, but I kick my foot against the desk to keep the door secure. "Please let me in, hon." I pick up my wooden crucifix and stare into Jesus, hoping he can sense my rage. "C'mon, babe, open up." I squeeze the crucifix as though wringing a neck. The wood begins to crack.

Where is your protection? I wonder. *Where is your salvation? WHERE ARE YOU?* I snap the cross in half and throw the pieces against the door.

Barry walks away.

I drop down on my bed and cover my head with my pillow. To lessen the ache of Sister Alice's death, I try thinking of the times she was mean to me, but can only come up with one. She yelled at me three years ago, after I first arrived, for eating the last of the peanut butter before I asked if anyone else wanted any. I was used to fending for myself. That was the lowest she made me feel, yet it was my fault and I learned a valuable lesson. Consequently, I have no choice but to feel every ounce of pain and scream into my pillow as loud as I can.

Around nine o'clock, I'm finally able to breathe in steady streams, and have managed to go a full minute without crying. When a tap sounds on my window, I immediately get the sense it's Dennis, even though that area was recently visited by something evil. To remain on the safe side I ask, "Who's there?"

"It's me," Dennis replies. "Can I come in?"

I remove the curtain rod from its brackets, unlock the window, and lift it open for him. Dennis shifts his legs inside and wriggles through on his back. He lands awkwardly, but I grab him to keep him from falling down. Once he steadies himself, I sit on the edge of my bed and watch him as he paces. "Sorry for the dramatics, but if Jeremy heard me coming in here—"

"She died screaming. I guess she wasn't enough of a priority to protect."

Dennis stops short and closes his eyes. He sits beside me and takes my hand. "Why Sister Alice?"

"So the rest of us have no safe haven to return to if he's caught? That's my only guess." I retrieve my hand from Dennis and fall back into my wet pillow. "Don't come near me. I'll only get you killed."

Dennis lies down beside me and nestles against my back. As I used to do with Sister Alice after having bad dreams, I wrap his arm around me and hold on tight to his hand. He pats my hair, which starts me crying again.

CHAPTER VI

I awaken in the morning to find my desk moved aside enough for Dennis to have slipped past. A note beside my pillow reads, "Hey, Robin, I'll be out and about keeping Jeremy away from you. I'll try to rent something for you and me for later. I hope you're feeling better. Dennis." Though I'd rather have his company, as the recollection of Sister Alice's demise is already hammering my guts, I appreciate his running interference to make my day a little easier.

When I climb out of bed I notice the crucifix I broke last night, but feel no remorse. Though the sharp edges could probably fit together evenly, I'd rather not mend them. If I have to live in a broken state, so too does my representation of Christ.

With nothing to do but wallow alone, I go outside in my bikini and sit by the pool. The temperature has risen considerably, and the humidity has thickened. Though my fear of death has been amplified, I decide to go in the water on my own so I won't perish without ever having done so. I step down the ladder one rung at a time, allowing each part of my body adjust to the cold, and I never let go of the handles. When submerged, I extend my legs so that I can float and feel as spirits must feel when they drift toward their ethereal destination.

Once my fingertips begin to curl, I sit on the deck and stare into the water. The sun streaks on the surface resemble lightening overlaying a blue sky. While in this trance, distracted from the pain of humankind, I hear the back door squeak open. I stand to leave, assuming Jeremy and Dennis have returned, but it's Barry who waddles toward the deck. He offers me a smile and says, "What are you up to?" When his eyes survey my near-naked body, I wrap myself in my towel. "What I mean to ask is, how are you feeling?"

"Not great," I reply. He waits for me to say more, but that's all I can manage.

"Well, I certainly can't heal your pain, but I bet I can ease it a bit." He removes two tickets from his vest pocket and holds them out to me. I instantly recognize the New York Mets logo. Although the sting of my mother figure's loss doesn't wane, the prospect of attending my first baseball game causes my heart to flutter.

"Thank you," I say. "I'll go get dressed."

After changing into a T-shirt and shorts, I go out front to meet Barry at his car. He's wearing a Yankees hat and jersey, which irks me to no end. I hope he gets beer cups thrown at him by the more unruly Mets fans.

The ride to Citi Field challenges my fear of dying at the hands of a silent murderer. Barry drives as though the other cars are motionless obstacles. He zigzags around slower vehicles so often that we never stay in one lane for more than a mile. If there's no room to move over, he'll ride magnetically close to other bumpers. He even uses the HOV lane without waiting for a legal entrance, and never seems to mind the barrage of honks and middle fingers that are directed his way. I can't tell if he's trying to beat traffic or the speed of light, but we do make it to Citi Field an hour before the first pitch.

After Barry begrudgingly shells out twenty-three dollars for parking, he pulls into a spot near an exit. Barry hands me sunglasses and a Yankees cap, which I refuse to wear, so he harrumphs and rummages around the floor of the backseat, finding a beige fishing hat that is truly atrocious—but better than a Yankees cap.

I step out, stretch my tensed back and legs, and

marvel at a stadium I've only seen on TV. The enormous home of the Mets vaunts sectioned glass within brick pillars, and resembles a modern Roman arena. Small trees and photos of historic players line smooth concrete paths around the venue. The home run apple from Shea Stadium is situated on a circular garden where couples and families are taking photographs together. Fanwalk bricks, where names of individual fans and families claim their allegiance, reside in patches outside the entrance gates. Sister Alice always wanted to get one for us, but the church never had the money to spare.

Barry keeps his hand on my back while I observe Citi Field's wondrous exterior, and he doesn't remove it until a security guard checks him for weapons with a metal rod. Once we walk through the turnstiles and into the crowded Jackie Robinson rotunda, his hand returns to my back and steers me toward an escalator. The Mets Hall of Fame is on the ground floor, and I'd love to go in, but I'm just as anxious to get to our seats and see the field.

We ride the escalator up to field level, and walk among a slow-moving crowd toward the faraway bullpen expanse. Souvenir stores and food stands line the barriers on our left, while seats and open glimpses of the playing area rest on our right. Once we cross the Shea Bridge, we meet an usher in a maroon polo shirt who escorts us halfway down his section to our seats.

Seeing the field in person for the first time makes my breath stammer. The group home TV isn't very big, and it in no way prepared me for how refined and vibrant the expansive grass is, nor how the dampened infield dirt appears smooth as velvet. I'm also thrilled to find we'll be sitting close to the newer home run apple, which is positioned upright for batting practice.

Barry sits beside me and puts his arm over the back of my chair. He isn't touching me, but just in case he decides to I lean forward to watch the visiting Dodgers stretch on the outfield grass. Some of their players are close enough to toss balls to the kids bent over the right field fence. The children who catch the balls seem overjoyed, even though their souvenirs have come from the opposition.

When catching a whiff of nearby fast food vendors, Barry sniffs at the air like a famished dog and says, "Hungry?"

"Starving," I say, as the comfort of the stadium allows me to consider food. "I hear the Shake Shack burgers are really good."

"From who? The guy who owns Shake Shack?"

"The announcers."

"Like they wouldn't have anything invested."

"It's right around the corner."

"Fine. Anything to drink?"

"Sprite, please."

"Sit tight, and don't leave for anything in the world. I have to crap like a goose, then I'll grab us some food."

Lovely. As soon as he leaves, I sit back with my eyes closed and breathe in the air of a place I'm glad to see before I die. I lay a hand over my crucifix charm, which I still wear—not because I'm thrilled with God, but because Sister Alice gave it to me on my first Holy Communion and I haven't taken it off since. Upon doing so, a warm and steady breeze sails across me. I can only hope it's a sign that God is real, that Sister Alice made it to Heaven, and that she and I can spend time at Citi Field together.

Barry returns forty minutes later with a cardboard box packed with four burgers, two hot dogs, and two drinks. He squeezes himself into his seat, hands me a cup of Sprite, and slides a dark cola into his own cup holder. He hands me a hot dog and burger and sets the box down at his feet, just as the announcer tells us to rise and remove our caps for the singing of the National Anthem. I put my food on my seat after I stand, but Barry is so intent on eating he ignores the directive. By the time the song ends, Barry has already eaten two hamburgers.

"I hate to admit it," he says, "but those announcers are right." He unleashes a crackling burp that has people looking toward us in horrified amazement. "Those were friggin' good!"

I sit back down and take a bite of my own burger and, sure enough, the Shake Shack burgers live up to their hype.

The Mets take the field by the time I finish eating. I stand and applaud, although everyone else around me remains seated. Watching the Mets run to their respective positions is an incomparable thrill. When the Mets pitcher throws his first warm up pitch, I slide to the edge of my seat. Barry's hand lands between my shoulders. He leans into me and says, "I'll bet you five bucks the Mets lose by seven."

"You're nuts," I say. "The Dodgers' pitcher has a high-four ERA on the road." He sits back with a shrug and keeps his hand on me. When the lead off batter steps to the plate, Barry begins tracing my spine with his fingertips. I try guessing the pitch selection as a means to ignore him, but his fingers keep descending. When he reaches my tail bone, I lean back hard, whether I crush his bones or not. Barry yanks his hand away just in time, with a playful laugh, then drops his palm onto my knee. His fingers skate to the hip-line of my shorts, and slide forward again. I try not to shudder.

"Please don't do that," I say, my voice tight and threatening. Barry gazes at me as if he has no idea what I'm talking about, but I know full well. My mother brought home plenty of men like him, and even though only one of them went too far, that one was enough.

The Mets threaten to score in the bottom of the inning, helping me dismiss Barry's persistent creepiness. With a runner on third and two out, their power batter steps to the plate. Three pitches later, he strikes out swinging on a breaking pitch in the dirt. I feel Sister Alice's vigor flow through me and I shout, "For the love of Saint Lucia, lay off the sinkers!"

An usher carrying a hot dog container looks at me confusedly. He clearly doesn't know Saint Lucia is savior of the blind.

Barry puts his hand on my thigh again and says, "I have to tell you: this place is a joke, but you're much better company than my wife. I tried taking her to a Yankees game last year, but she just sulked the whole time."

Though I want to remain distracted from his every movement and breath, he's broken my concentration with a problem I want rectified. "Why doesn't she like me?"

He takes my left hand and holds it in his lap. My fingertips immediately prune from his hot, sweaty palm. "Don't take offense, honey. She doesn't like anybody. Or anything. And I mean anything." He laughs and moves my hand further up his thigh, which is closer than I'd like for it to travel. I whip my hand away and place it between my knees.

"Something the matter?" he asks.

"I'm sorry, but I'm not big on people touching me."

"But you'll lie in bed with Dennis."

"That's different. He doesn't grope."

"Oh, really? I grope?" He looks straight at me awaiting a response, but I don't know how to explain myself without offending him. My slight physical contact with Dennis seems perfectly natural and a result of the friendship between us. Barry's touches are uninvited intrusions. Having waited too long for an answer, Barry tries to readjust himself so that his back is to me, but the seat is too small and he barely budges. "I try so hard to please you, Robin, but I can't seem to do anything right."

"I appreciate the gestures, sir."

"Sir." Barry folds his short arms over his gut.

"She'll go to a game I drive her to, as long as I don't lay a fat finger on her." His face reddens and his bottom eyelids moisten. He looks legitimately hurt, but I can't tell if it's a ruse to get me to beg for forgiveness. With the way things are going in my life, I can only assume his motives are for the worse, so I remain quiet.

Barry doesn't speak to me on the ride home (after a grueling Mets loss) to keep up with the silent treatment he managed during the game. I think he's coming around when he stops off at a convenience store, but he leaves with only one bagged ice cream cone that he eats in six bites. When we arrive back at the house, I thank him for the game, but he heads straight inside without looking back.

On the way to my room, I pause as I hear another bizarre recitation coming from beyond Jeremy's door. In a baritone voice he chants, "The dripping of the nectar from my eager cleft!"

Though lights are on in Dennis's room, I don't want to ruin his evening by releasing my frustrations on him, so I plunge onto my bed and wring my pillow to will away the anger brought upon by Barry, and the way the Mets game ended. Seconds later, Dennis knocks on my door frame and says, "I watched the highlights on the news. The Mets got screwed on that call."

"I could tell he was safe from four hundred feet away," I say. "That was bullshit."

Dennis backs into the door, eyes aghast. "If that was your first curse, I'm flattered, but it's just a game—"

"That I'd like to forget about." I roll onto my stomach and stuff my head in my pillow. Dennis lies on his stomach beside me and makes sure our arms touch.

"This can't be about a blind ump and a faulty replay system. What did Barry do?"

I turn sideways to grab at him while deepening my voice in imitation to say, "My wife won't play with me anymore."

Dennis sits up, holds my hands still, and looks at me with humorless concern. "He touched you?"

I maneuver to sit Indian style. "Nothing explicit. I think he's just . . . needy."

"Maybe the pervert should focus on his wife and keep his needy hands off you!" Dennis squeezes his right hand into a fist and looks around as though he has to punch something to quell his anger. Instead, he unties the lace on my left sneaker.

"Is that why Lori is mean to me? Because I'm the center of his attention?"

He hisses while bearing his bottom teeth, which

stretches his lip and causes the scab to break and bleed. He jumps up, checks the hallway, closes the door tight, sits close to me, and whispers, "I don't think they'd want you to know this." I wipe away the blood on his chin with my thumb, carefully, so I don't cause him pain. His eyes shift to my shoe and he begins tying up the lace. "I looked them up when they took me in and found a few articles online. About five years ago, Lori and Barry had a four-month-old daughter who died from crib death." My right hand lands over my crucifix charm while my lower guts churn. "If that wasn't enough, it happened the night before she was supposed to be baptized."

"Baptized? Here?"

"From what I've picked up on, Lori was raised Catholic. She married into a family who haven't been fans of the church for a long time. Once her daughter died she turned her back on religion too. I'm surprised they took you in, considering where you come from."

"But why do Barry and Lori hate each other?"

"He wanted another kid, but she didn't. She agreed to sign adoption papers, which is how me and Jeremy got here, but I think it was just to keep him off her back about having their own. Four years have gone by and she's barely spoken to me. Neither has Barry, for that matter. Not that I mind. This place beats an orphanage. *Lights out at nine o'clock, Dennis! No horror movies in the rec room, Dennis!*"

"How did you end up . . . alone?" This is a long overdue question, but not one I would ask if I didn't think Dennis confided in me enough to answer.

"My parents died in a car crash. I survived in the backseat. I have no other family, so that was that."

"And Jeremy?"

"His parents left him in the woods with a sign that read *EAT ME.*"

I laugh so abruptly I accidentally spit on his forearm. He wipes it off on my sheets without making it an issue. "I actually don't know his story. I asked once, but he doesn't speak unless he's ranting. How'd you end up with Sister Alice?"

I pull off my left sneaker, because Dennis tied it too tight, then kick off the other. "One of my mother's boyfriends thought it would be fun to take my virginity, but he was drunk enough that I was able to fight him off. He still beat me up so badly that the school nurse found blood in my ears the next day. I could have lied about what happened to protect Mom, but I'd had enough of living in random places, eating scraps for dinner, and having her men look at me like I'm a toy. The nurse called CPS, and the next day I was in the group home."

"I'm sorry for why you ended up here, but I'm glad I got to know you. There's never been anyone to talk to. The video store clerk is the closest I have to a friend." He looks away with sadness, maybe realizing I'll have to leave once the killer is apprehended. There's nothing I can say to console him, because if that's what he's thinking, he's right. "I rented you a present. I'm not sure what it's about. I picked it out because of the title. Come look."

He kisses me on the cheek, which feels surprisingly natural, and stands with my hand in his.

We go to his room, where he digs through a bag of video rentals and hands me one that looks far from comforting. The cover presents a knife wedged into the bleeding torso of a baby doll. The title, however, reads *Alice Sweet Alice*. I agree to watch as long as Jeremy doesn't decide to join us, and we hear him leave while Dennis is loading the movie. My bizarre night is suddenly looking brighter.

Alice Sweet Alice centers on a troubled brat named, no big surprise, Alice, who's the main suspect in the death of her sister, Karen. Karen is murdered in church moments before her first holy communion. Strangely, neither the sight of Karen's smoldering corpse, nor a bloody stairway stabbing, nor the plummeting demise of a generally kind character discourage me from watching. After witnessing Sister Alice in her final condition, nothing fabricated on film will ever upset me again.

When the movie ends, I swing my feet off the bed and stretch as hard as I can. Having sat in a car for nearly two hours round trip, and in the Citi Field seat for three, my back muscles have stiffened and ache. "Will you be up for a while if I can't fall asleep?" I ask.

"If I'm out just wake me up," he replies.

I blow him a quick kiss that he catches and slaps on his cheek.

Alone in bed, shrouded by darkness, I focus on the positive aspects of the Mets game (mainly that I went at all), and this quality time with Dennis. My mind, however, keeps returning to Sister Alice, and the wonder of how I'll manage to get through her wake tomorrow afternoon without completely breaking down. I can't stop picturing her corpse, nor my travels through the group home basement.

In the comfort of my imagination, I allow myself to enter the cellar again, where I'm drawn to the crackling under the stairs. Rather than focus on finding the staircase itself, I inch closer to the origin of the sounds; the mannequin in the habit. The nearer I get, the more I'm able to pick up noises I didn't pay attention to last night, notably the frenetic breathing of someone trying to contain their laughter. When I reach the open partition, my eyes focus deep into the nun's murky headdress. Within the hood I discover Jeremy's vile grin.

I sit up abruptly and try to convince myself I'm only seeing what my mind fears—even though Jeremy could be the perpetrator, with his relentless anger, his satanic leanings, and his cruelty toward his adoptive family. I've only known him for a few days, but have seen more hostility in him than any of the bullies in school I've known for years. To set my mind at ease, there's only one thing I can do. I have to search Jeremy's room.

With all the courage I can muster, I tiptoe out of bed and open my door for a peek into the hall. Jeremy's bedroom door is closed and his lights are off. I creep nearer, wondering if I should ask Dennis to keep a lookout for me, but he could be asleep and I don't want to involve him in what could be my own delusions.

After jiggling Jeremy's doorknob, and hearing no response at all, I open the door a crack. I slowly reach inside, turn on a light, and exhale through puckered lips when finding the room empty. The decorations, however, tighten my stomach.

Jeremy's bedroom is covered with posters of the bands whose wild, angry music pulsates all day through the walls. Their logos are of satanic carvings, revolting creatures, and a blasphemous red idol. A skull I hope is plastic rests atop his dresser amid melted black candles, a silver chalice, and a bronze bell. A small gold tray holds long strands of hair that he must have extracted from my comb. *The Satanic Bible* rests near these implements of evil, which is opened to a ritual called "Invocation of Lust." My rattling fingers suggest I should leave, but I feel I'm getting closer to singling out something important.

When I open Jeremy's closet door I'm taken aback by a strong smell. Atop of pile of pornographic magazines is an open cigar box that holds dried green leaves that look like spices, and hand rolled cigarettes that look like thick, white worms. Black shirts are lined up on the hangers. I kneel to move aside a cardboard box from the back corner, to see if can find a nun's habit, clothes that smell of gasoline, or tools that could extract eyes. While digging about, a shadow emerges behind me.

"Looking for something?" Jeremy says. An icy chill whips up my spine and locks me in place. I try to think of an excuse as to why I'm rummaging through his belongings, but I can barely breathe, let alone in-vent a believable lie. Before I can consider how to get away from him, he pins me between his calves at my waist and unzips his pants. "Bathe in the nectar of your new god, bitch."

A warm surge of urine is unleashed upon the back of my head. Jeremy pivots from side to side to douse my ears. Streams run into and burn my eyes. He squeezes his legs tighter while forcing a heavy gush between my shoulder blades. I don't think he'll ever stop, but he's suddenly jerked away.

I look back, allowing pooled liquid to empty from my left ear, and watch Dennis lift Jeremy sideways and slam him to the floor. Dennis never utters a word, but the creases in his face suggest total fury as he relentlessly punches Jeremy in the head and chest. Jeremy squirms and howls, but can provide no defense to a beating he so richly deserves.

I work up the strength to stand on wobbly legs and rush into the bathroom. I pry off my saturated shirt and drop it into the sink where it lands with a splat. I strip naked, hop into the shower, and spin the hot valve four rotations. I tinker with the cold valve just enough so I won't sear off my skin.

After close to an hour of washing and rewashing my hair, I peek into the hall for Jeremy, hurry into my room to change into spare pajamas, peek into the hall for Jeremy, and head into Dennis's room. He's laying on top of the bedding, staring at the ceiling. I lie down beside him, but neither of us speak. I move his arm around me and rest my head on his chest to listen to his heart.

Sometime after midnight, I'm awakened by heavy breathing. I open my eyes to a looming silhouette, and grip the sheets in fear of Jeremy's reprisal, but it's Barry who grabs my arm and yanks me off the bed. He lifts me onto his shoulder, carries me to my room, drops me down on my mattress and says, "Sleep in your own goddamned room!" He slams my door shut and lumbers away.

Somewhere within the darkness, perhaps from my closet, underneath my bed, or outside my window, I hear laughter. I can't help but feel the taunt is coming from God.

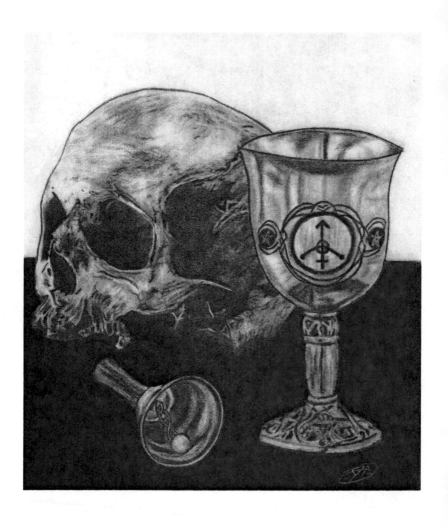

CHAPTER VII

Grumbling voices in the hallway awaken me. At first I put my pillow over my head so I can continue sleeping, but when recalling the beating Jeremy received, I sit up to listen. "The way you and Robin act around each other is disgusting," Barry is saying, "and look what it led to! Jeremy can't even open his eyes!"

"Did he tell you what he did to her?" Dennis asks.

"What was she doing in his room?"

Jeremy, through undoubtedly swollen lips, chimes in with, "Shuh a crothe uh huh ath!"

"Jesus Christ," Barry continues, "he can't even speak English. I don't want to see either of your faces for the rest of my day off! In your rooms! *Now!*"

Dennis and Jeremy exchange heated words before each of their doors bangs shut. Barry's footsteps land in front of my room. I pull the covers to my chin in case he decides to come in, but he ultimately walks away.

I remain in bed until my stomach calms, and decide to go upstairs to apologize to Barry for the rift I've created between him and his adoptive sons. I need him to drive me to Sister Alice's wake today, and don't want his bad mood to prevent me from attending.

I stand before Barry's den for a few moments, building up the courage to knock, but hesitate when I hear a voice from the room across the hall. Lori is speaking in such a joyful tone that I feel the need to inspect what she's saying and, more importantly, who she's saying it to. The door to what appears a master bedroom is half-open, allowing me a view of the rocking chair she's sitting in. Her back is facing me, but I can tell she's reading from a sizable picture book.

"*Presently along came a wolf,*" Lori says. "*He knocked on the door and said, 'Little pig, little pig, let me come in!' To which the pig answered—*"

A child's nasally voice replies, "*Not by the hair of my chinny chin chin!*" Hearing delight in Lori's presence wrenches me upright. I haven't a clue whose child is meeting her favor, since visitors never stop by, and she doesn't appear to have any friends. She either babysits, has another child I wasn't told about, or has taken up kidnapping.

"*The wolf then answered to that, 'Then I'll huff and I'll puff and I'll blow your house in!' So he huffed and he puffed and he blew his house in, and ate up the little pig.*" Lori leans forward and rustles up the bed sheets while growling like a wolf. The child I can't see playfully shrieks. Lori sits back, but keeps the chair from rocking by grounding her toes. "*The second little pig met a man with a bundle of furze and said—*"

"What's furze?" the child wonders.

"Sticks. *The pig met the man with sticks and said, 'Please, man, give me those sticks to build a house,' which the man did, and the pig built his house.*" I inch into the room far enough to glance over Lori's shoulder. Under the sheets of a twin bed, of which there are two separated by a night stand, is a lump too small to be a child old enough to speak. "*Then along came the wolf who said, 'Little pig, little pig, let me come in.'*"

I know better than to press my luck with someone as snippy as Lori, but too many awful things are happening to children and I can't ignore something this strange. I open the door a few more inches for a clearer look at the bed. When my eyes meet her listener, a porcelain doll with vibrant green eyes, I suck in a sharp breath. Lori jumps out of the chair, making it rock full tilt, and claps the book to her chest. "What are you doing in here?" she snaps.

"I'm looking for Barry," I reply.

"He's in his den, oblivious to the real world! Where else would he be? In here is where we deal with matters of life and death!" Tears brew in her frenzied eyes, so I back into the hallway until I bump into a cushion that smells like nachos.

Barry takes me by the wrist, pulls me into his room, and closes the door. He drops into his recliner, mutes the volume of a sports talk show, and says to me, "Don't worry about Lori. Frankly, she's out of her mind and I'm tired of dealing with her." I sit at the edge of the folding chair, slightly eased by his aware-ness of her. "And don't think I'm going to come down on you for breaking rules I never set, but I'm officially forbidding you from spending time in Dennis's room with no supervision. You're both of that age where boys and girls get into . . . filth. I can't allow it."

"I'm sorry," I say, "but I don't always feel safe by myself."

Barry shifts toward me and puts his hands on my knees. "You can come to me for that kind of comfort, honey. Nobody can protect you the way I can. I have proof."

He jerks himself out of the chair and goes into a closet that's packed with oversized Yankees shirts and sweaters. He retrieves a long case from the floor that resembles a keyboard cover. Barry flips open the long lid and lifts out an instrument that renders a completely different tune: a black shotgun. I lean back against the chair as far as I can without pressing myself through the breach.

Barry smirks proudly and says, "If you ever run into trouble, and I'm not here, this is what you do." He removes a shell from within the case and slides it into a metal trap on the underside of the gun. After pumping the handle with significant force, he aims the barrel at the door. "Presto! Just like that you're ready to defend yourself. You just have to make sure this little doohickey isn't red or you won't be shooting anyone." He's referring to the safety catch near the trigger guard. "Remember, I'm only showing you this as a last resort. I don't want to find you up here playing with it."

"You don't have to worry about that."

He puts the gun down, kneels before me, and takes my hands into his; the way men do when they propose marriage. "I only want what's best for you, Robin." He leans in to hug me, but I put my hands on his shoulders and press him away. I thought I made it clear that I've had enough of his advances.

"You can help without touching me."

He lifts himself up with difficultly, almost falling

over, while his eyes squint with anger. "I heard about your situation and volunteered to protect any one of you kids. Sorry for giving a shit."

Sweating and huffing, he drops into his chair, grabs a fistful of chips from a snack tray, and stuffs them into his mouth. I almost speak because he looks so upset, but think better of it because I'm still not sure of his intentions. Not eager to dig into his psyche, I change the subject and say in a friendly tone, "The first viewing for Sister Alice is at two. Will you be able—"

"Don't worry, your highness. Your chauffeur will be ready."

I murmur a thank you and head downstairs for a drink. The tension from my encounter with Lori, and then Barry, have parched my throat. When I step into the kitchen, I stop short when I find Jeremy at the refrigerator. He looks directly at me, although I'm not certain how much he can see since his eyes are nearly swollen shut. Through bloated, purple lips he says, "Huck hou, hurrahucker!" I speed past him and decide to get water from the downstairs sink.

I want to see what Dennis is up to, and to tell him about my brushes with his adoptive parents, but Jeremy follows me downstairs and watches until I enter my room. For the rest of the morning and early afternoon he plays sentinel to Dennis and myself. Every time one of our doors opens, Jeremy rushes out of his room hollering something nonsensical about us remaining apart. I'd ignore him, but don't want him to bring Barry down here in fear he'd retract his offer to take me to the wake.

To pass time, I try on the outfits Barry brought for me to wear to church. The only black item is a form fitting dress. It's a bit too revealing, but I have no other clothes—I'm certainly not going to ask Barry to take me shopping.

At a quarter past one, as I begin to get antsy, a hard knock sounds on my door and Barry yells, "Let's get this over with!"

I take a deep breath, to build courage to face him and the funeral home, and open the door. Barry's wearing black pants and a black sweater that's been washed so many times it's covered with gray fuzz. At first he appears angry, but when he looks me over with devouring eyes he smiles and says, "Tight!" Apparently, he hasn't become a gentleman since we last met.

Dennis comes out of his room in black dress pants and a dark red dress shirt. Barry grinds his teeth until the veins on his temples throb, and says rather calmly, "Back in your room."

"Are you serious?" Dennis says. "It's a wake."

"You should have thought about that before you used your brother as a Bop Bag."

"You're kidding me. How can you not let—"

Barry expels a sharp "*NO!*" that bounces off the walls and shoots straight through my ears. Dennis, unwilling to put up a fight, goes back in his room with a subdued groan. I can't say I'm not disappointed, but I guess surrendering is easier than engaging in a fight he most likely couldn't win.

The Scrimm Funeral Parlor is a small white building just down the street from the Holy Sepulcher Cemetery where Sister Alice will be buried. Black appareled men and women, many of whom I recognize from my church, are gloomily arriving or leaving. Their postures and facial expressions are of complete desolation. I'm skeptical of people I'm not familiar with, and realize the killer could be scouting the wake for me. It might not be the greatest idea to have come, but if the perpetrator has my address anyway, I might as well let him end me wherever he wants.

Inside, a maroon carpeted lobby breaks off into two hallways. The right side leads to a door that's blocked off by a velvet rope. The left side leads to an open door beside a letter board that reads: *Sister*

Alice Beatrice Aloia. I exhale a fraction of my pent-up sorrow, and walk toward the room on rickety legs. Barry is close enough to lean on, but I'm not going to use him for physical support. Luckily, the crowd in the viewing room is so abundant I'm able to lose him when squeezing through.

While locating the closed casket at the far end, I can't help but notice that anyone who looks at me does so with worry. Those who know I'm a group home child must realize I've lost my role model, and are probably taking in their last glimpse of someone whose funeral they also might soon attend. I don't regard them for long. Once I catch the foot end of a shiny wooden coffin, I put my crucifix charm in my mouth and proceed.

A nun is kneeling and praying at the head of the casket. She finishes by kissing her fingers and touching them to the fastened lid. An older man on deck is about to pay his respects, but when he sees me approaching he motions for me to cut ahead. I can't even speak to thank him, but I do feel gracious.

I kneel on a padded beam before the casket, clasp my hands in prayer, and recite an "Our Father." When finished, I open my eyes to polished oak and wish I could see Sister Alice one last time in a peaceful state, to dispel the horrible sight of her in agony. While thinking of what to say, I begin twisting my crucifix between my fingers.

"I always knew this day had to come," I eventually whisper, "but not like this." Tears warm my cheeks in straight trails. I wipe them off, and glance back at the line of mourners growing behind me. "I'm glad my mother wasn't interested in me. I can't imagine my life without you. I would just appreciate a sign so I know you're in safe hands, and that God's kingdom exists, and that what happened to you can't get in the way of how much love you can still provide for this world. If God's at your side, maybe you can convince Him to call off whatever He's been up to. If anything, for Amanda."

I begin crying so hard that someone behind me puts a tissue in my hand. I nod with gratitude and dry my eyes and nose. "I should go. You have a lot of friends who want to say goodbye. I want you to know I love you . . . and I'm really going to miss you." I kiss the casket, wipe my tears off the polish, and turn around to see proof that the virtue in Sister Alice has already found its way to me.

A slim divide in the crowd allows me to see Dennis standing in the back, near the entryway. He's sweaty and out of breath, as though he rode his bike a million miles an hour to get here. He gently eases his way through the gathering and meets me with a gentle hug. I close my eyes and absorb his warmth. When I softly back away, I notice Barry watching us from a corner chair. He says words to himself that look nowhere near compassionate, but I haven't a care in the world about him.

Dennis and I sit side by side throughout the wake, while Barry wanders in and out of the room to make sure we see him checking his watch. A few people approach me to extend their condolences, and to tell me I'm in their hearts and prayers. I appreciate their kindness, but in a room fronted by death, I wonder deep down if their prayers will save anyone.

Later that night, Dennis falls asleep halfway through a movie, which is a luxury that won't befall me. I try going to bed, but my stomach is too sour. To distract the constant waves of pain, I decide to go outside, killer be damned.

While gently rocking on one of the backyard swings, I envision my life without Sister Alice, but can't picture myself growing old. My mind refuses to conceive of a future, as though I'm doomed to a short existence.

The back screen door squeaks open. A silhouette nears, and I never doubt it's anyone but Dennis. He appears through clouded moonlight, sits on the swing beside me, and rocks from left to right to get his seat to bang against mine. I sway my seat against his until we build enough speed to nearly knock each others teeth loose. After a hushed laugh, Dennis hops up and stands before me. He grabs the chains just above my hands, holds me still, and leans his face toward mine. I tilt my head to the side, because that's how I've seen people kiss on TV. His lips meet mine without our noses getting in the way and linger for a few moments. We then lean our foreheads together. I think he says something, but my heartbeat is clogging my ears.

We stay outside a little longer, not making a sound, until a light upstairs goes on. Figuring it's best to not get caught out here, we go back down to our rooms and bid each other good night with soft pecks on the lips.

Alone in the dark, the grueling pain of Sister Alice's loss continues to hound me. When I think of Dennis, a stream of prickles flow down from my cheeks, up from my toes, and settle on a precise spot beneath my waist. I reach under my pajama bottoms to explore the source with cautious fingers, and am instantly aroused by a warm twinge. I think to extract my hand, since I know I'm up to something sinful, but if God hadn't intended me to do such a thing, He would never have invented the spot to begin with.

My fingers rub the swelling knot with exceeding speed. I part my shivering knees to allow my hand freedom to gyrate. A burst of elation creeps up to my throat and causes me to squeal. I turn my face into my pillow while pressing my fingers down harder and circling them faster. My entire body stiffens with numb surges. My thoughts of God and despair completely vanish when I envision Dennis holding me, Dennis kissing me, and Dennis shirtless on my bed as we partake in things prohibited until marriage. Before long, I explode at the mid. My toes curl and my fingertips warm with a sticky gush of release. My knees connect hard as I lift my backside to squeeze out every ounce of pain I've felt in the past several weeks.

Panting atop my bed, my head still deep in my pillow, I hear a shuffle in my closet. I whip my hand out of my pants and listen intently to the clicking of hangers. God forbid I have one moment of uninterrupted peace in this place.

When the clacking continues, I worry Nathan has come down in his delusional state again. I step out of bed and turn on the light, which shocks my eyes closed. I hear the closet door opening and something dropping to the floor. Through blurred vision I make out Kermit the Frog slippers, a pink nightgown, and blond hair that's caked to the cheeks of what appears a life-sized doll. As I inch closer, and my eyes gradually adapt, I recognize the doll as the lifeless body of my roommate, Amanda. My stomach explodes with scorching bile that incinerate my thrashing butterflies. I squeeze my pajama shirt to hold back a seething scream.

The closest door fully opens. Standing inside is a nun. She parts a dry mass of gray, bloodstained hair with each of her index fingers, exposing a wrinkled face. She opens one gray eye. Her left eye remains closed. She smiles with two teeth that protrude over her bottom lip. She's Gail Grantham, Nathan's invalid wife of fifty-four years.

When Gail suddenly reaches for me, I rush out of the room and leap upstairs, two steps at a time. I yank open the front door and run to the center of the yard frantically waving my arms to summon the cops keeping watch. I ease when noticing an orange glow across the horizon, as though several houses are on fire at once. A thin veil of smoke that drifts from their vicinity conceals the stars. Emergency sirens sound from several vehicles and firehouses. It appears as though Armageddon has struck.

The officer who came into the house the other night jumps out from a white Toyota sedan down the street and rushes over to me with a hand over a hol-stered gun. "The killer's inside," I say to him, "she's downstairs."

He looks doubtful when asking, "She?" I nod once. The cop draws his gun and double-steps toward the house saying, "Wait right here!"

I have no intentions of waiting right here. I have to get Dennis.

I hurry back inside and stand at the basement door, listening for the hopeful sounds of Gail's cap-ture, but there aren't any. Instead, the cop pounds up the steps, recoils with alarm when seeing me and says, "There's a corpse and two sleeping boys down there, but no one else." A soft bang sounds above us, as though a door has been closed. The cop runs straight upstairs while I run straight down.

Dennis is half-awake in his bed, leaning up on his elbow. He worriedly asks, "What's with the flashlight?"

"That cop is back," I answer, "the killer's in the house." I grab his hand and pull him to my room, where I cover Amanda with my bed sheets, sign the cross, and grab the top half of my broken wooden crucifix. If Jesus is ever going to protect me, the sharp end of his fractured post will have to do.

I hold the cross outward as Dennis follows me up to the dining room. A thud from upstairs causes the chandelier to rattle. A shrill scream is cut immediately short, as though someone were subdued in a heart-beat. I can't tell if it's a man or a woman.

Though standing close to safety, I'm afraid the cop is in trouble, and if that's the case, then I'm the one who sent him to his peril. Unwilling to spend the rest of my days living in fear for my own mortality, or guilt of a cop's death, I carefully inch my way up the stairs. Dennis never falls a step behind.

At the end of the unlit hall, Gail is squatting over the cop. A slurping sound carries from them, and it looks as though she's pulling out his eye with her fingers. When Dennis turns on a light, Gail looks at us sharply and hisses.

Dennis takes the crucifix from my hand and throws it at her, perhaps expecting it to pierce her sternum as it might in a movie, but it bounces off a wall and lands behind her. Gail cackles and stands with crooked jerks, as though her backbone is made of rusty gears. By the time I notice she's holding the cop's gun, she has it aimed at us.

Dennis shoves me into Barry's den, jumps in be-hind me, and elbows the door shut. He locks the knob and slides the recliner against the jambs. I listen for footsteps in the hall, while Dennis goes into the closet for the shotgun case. He extracts the weapon, thrusts in two shells, pumps the handle, and unclasps the safety.

"You've used that before?" I ask.

"I've pretended to," he replies, "I basically know what—" The doorknob jiggles. Dennis winces and pulls the trigger. The barrel explodes. The top of the recliner bursts into a cloud of cotton while a jagged hole tears through the center of the door. A body in the hall collapses with a grunt. Dennis pumps another shell into the chamber. His hands are shaking so badly the handle rattles. I lean close to the damaged door, listening to whether Gail has been fatally shot or merely wounded.

Barry sits up and peers through the smoldering hole with pained eyes that lock onto Dennis. "You vicious little shit," he says, and presses himself against the door with a violent surge, forcing the lock mechanism through the frame while sliding back the recliner. He steps inside and stares Dennis down while breathing like an asthmatic. Black holes in the stomach area of his pajama shirt run lines of dark blood. He grins shrewdly and says to me, "Don't worry, sugar. I won't let him get you too."

Dennis backs into a row of shelves and says, "It was an accident! I thought you were Gail!"

"Is this what you learned from that ghoul shit you

watch? How to kill women and children?"

"You don't understand," I say to Barry, "your mother's stroke was a trick." He doesn't hear me, or doesn't want to. Barry charges at Dennis shoulder first and slams him into the wooden ledges. Yankees junk topples to the floor. Dennis plummets with them. Barry retrieves the shotgun and looks down upon Dennis with a proud huff. Dennis gradually stands upright with wrathful eyes fixed on his adoptive father.

"That was the last time you'll ever touch me," Dennis says.

Barry laughs with, "Is that a fact?" He smacks Dennis across the face, leaving four bloody finger streaks on his cheek and brow. Dennis looks down with a snide grin and, as though remembering every verbal and physical blow he's taken since my arrival, hammers Barry's wounded stomach with a taut fist. Barry hunches over and screams through clenched teeth. Blood froths at the corners of his mouth. Dennis looks far from satisfied, though. His eyes widen with fright when seeing something behind me.

Before I can turn, a sharp implement is jammed through the arc of my right knee. I collapse with a shriek and find my crucifix embedded in my leg. Gail steps over me with her right eye in sinister concentration. The cop's eyeball is jammed crookedly into her empty left socket. The barrel of the pistol is staring directly at my chest.

I look to Dennis, who's desperately trying to wrangle the gun from his father's grasp, but Barry, unaware of my plight, throws him to the floor with a maniacal laugh. He looks at me with beaming pride, and notices his mother. Barry's eyes bulge out. He clutches his left arm and unleashes a chunky stream of vomit. The room is immediately smothered by an acidic stench. Barry, undoubtedly having a coronary, collapses on top of Dennis, who squeals as his lungs are emptied of air.

Gail sniffs up the pungent aroma, and exhales with a delighted hum. I try as nonchalantly as I can to crawl to the shotgun without her noticing, but she snatches it up with a victorious screech. She tucks the pistol into her belt of rosaries, and turns the shotgun on me. I shuffle away from Dennis, to save him from the buckshot, and pray for a miracle. To my surprise, Jeremy steps in the doorway, surveying the havoc. I expect him to cheer Gail on, but he appears genuinely terrified of her.

Gail follows my eyes to Jeremy and turns the gun his way. He ducks and scampers toward the stairs. She shoots at the doorway, perhaps hoping to nail him through the wall, but his footsteps bang down the staircase and head out the front door. Jeremy has escaped. Perhaps his god is more protective than mine.

Gail pumps the shotgun, but there isn't another shell for the chamber. She tosses it aside with a frustrated growl. I try prying the crucifix from my leg, but give up when the wood scrapes bone. Gail waves a pointer at me, steps onto my punctured leg, and plucks out the cross with a powerful thrust. She squats on my waist and, before I can maneuver to protect myself, drives the tip straight through my collar bone. I open my mouth to scream, but can only gasp through the pain.

Gail stares directly at me while baring her rotten teeth. She removes the cop's eyeball from her socket, holds it near my face, and squeezes. A light brown cornea slips between two fingers while a glob of clear liquid squirts through her thumb. She leans close to my face and slowly exhales hot breath that smells of baby food. She holds open her left eyelid, exposing an empty socket. Her orbital hole has been filled with some sort of cement. "Father Vincent did this to me," she says, her voice coarse and shrill. "You have him to thank."

Gail yanks the cross from my shoulder and matches the now-dull point to my left eye with an eagerness to plunge, but not everyone in the room is apt to see me die. Dennis howls, while rolling Barry's limp body off himself. His face has turned a muted purple, his lips are dull blue, but his bright eyes are fixated on Gail. She reaches for the handgun, but when the eyeball residue on her fingers prevents her from getting a firm grip, she hops up, grabs the empty shotgun, and limps into the hall.

Dennis finally is able to get out from under Barry's massive weight and crawls to the door to check for Gail. He bangs an open hand against the floor, scrambles over to me and says, "I don't see her."

"She has both guns," I say, "I'd rather not wait for her to come back and use them."

Dennis helps me stand on my good leg, wraps my good arm around his shoulders, and carries me to the stairs where we head down one step at a time. Certain Gail will emerge for a final jolt, we look behind us after every movement. When we reach the final step, a hand shoots through the banister rails and grabs my pajama pants. I kick it away with a scream, but Nathan reaches back through the bars and grabs both our legs.

"I've got them," Nathan says, "get back in here!" He looks around fearfully, as though he has no intention of harming us himself.

Dennis lets go of me, spins around the railing, and

pins Nathan against a wall with a forearm against his neck. "You've been helping her?" he asks.

Nathan tries to speak, but can only wheeze, so Dennis retracts his arm a bit. "She hasn't done anything on her own since she was crippled by that priest! The same priest who took over a church and had a group home named after him! How is that fair? Can't you see God punishes no one? Can't you see Robin and those other kids have to pay for his sins?"

Dennis pulls Nathan forward, puts a flat hand against his forehead, and slams him back into the wall. His head remains embedded in sheet rock. Dennis pulls him out and tosses him to the floor. Nathan lands, stiff and soundless.

After grabbing Barry's car keys off a hook near the door, Dennis walks me outside. The skyline is no longer glowing, but the stars are still hindered by smoke. Dennis helps me into the passenger seat, where I smear blood across the tan upholstery. As he runs to the driver's side, I notice Lori standing at the window of Barry's den. She's cradling her doll and making it wave goodbye at me.

Dennis climbs inside, slips the key into the ignition, and starts the engine. "You know how to drive?" I ask.

"First time for everything," he replies. He backs

out of the driveway, rolls over the curb, and jerks us to a stop. He recoils with shame, but eventually proceeds forward slow enough to maintain control. "Where to? Police station or hospital?"

"Head for the church."

"Why? You can't pray for stitches."

"We'll call for an ambulance there. I have to talk to the person who started all this before Gail moves on to his other congregants." Probably realizing there's no straight path to reason, Dennis heads toward the church.

While riding out of the neighborhood, we come upon Jeremy, who's running sloppily on the shoulder as though he's completely out of breath. Dennis appears too intent on driving to notice him, even as Jeremy stops to look at us when we pass. I'm not sure if he can see me in the darkness, but I show him my middle fingers anyway.

Father Vincent's rectory is behind the church parking lot, a small building fronted by orange bricks and slim windows. The foundation is lined with bushes and flowerbeds. Dennis lifts me out of the car and guides me up the three wooden steps to the front door. Though the pain in my shoulder and knee are making me lightheaded, I manage to ring the doorbell.

A few moments later, an old man in a dark red

bathrobe answers. Incapable of hiding his repulsion, he looks me over with gaping eyes and says, "God in Heaven! What happened to you?"

"We're looking for Father Vincent," I say.

"You should be looking for a hospital." He opens the door and helps me into a small vestibule where an empty coat rack stands beside a lenticular Shroud of Turin. Dennis leads me into a living room area and sits me down on a black leather couch. The blood flow from my leg seems to have lessened, but I still leave a spotted trail on the beige carpet. "Sit tight, I'll call an ambulance."

"Can you tell Father Vincent we're here?"

"I'm afraid he's not in a proper state of mind. I'm Father Desmond. I'll be more than happy to help you."

"Please. He's involved with what happened to us tonight. I'm the last orphan from his home."

"I'll tell him you're here, but I can't promise cohesion. He's been on something of a bender since the crimes began."

Father Desmond heads down a slender hallway. Two voices in conversation carry in from a further room. Father Vincent staggers into the living room wearing maroon pajamas and black slippers. His cheeks are red and his hair is uncombed, but his glassy eyes become fully attentive to my condition. He drops to his knees before me, but his hands linger as though searching for a spot to touch that isn't marred with blood.

"Who did this to you?" he asks.

I suck in a breath and, certain the news will stun him, expel, "Gail Grantham."

Father Vincent lets out a loud, strangely insincere laugh, but his eyes flood with worry. "That's impossible. She's my age and, last I heard, an invalid."

Father Desmond returns to us while clicking off a cordless phone. "Do you mean Gail Poerio," he asks, "the nun in training who jumped off a roof all those years ago?"

"Depends on who you believe," I reply, "some might say she's targeting the person who pushed her."

"You're delusional," Father Vincent says. He stands and careens to a booze-topped bar, pours himself a large glass of brandy, and sucks it down in three swallows. "How much blood have you lost exactly?"

"Do you think it's a coincidence the murders started when you were appointed to this church? You got away with a crime against her. She spent most of her life suffering while you continue receiving honors. She's destroying the children who lived under your name to absolve your sin."

Father Vincent rolls his eyes at the ceiling as if to act complacent, but his hands are shaking so badly he's forced to make fists. "The church and I aid in spiritual matters. I suggest you take this up with the police."

"Can't you make restitution with her while she's still alive?"

"How? I'm not in harm's way. She's hunting you kids."

"She killed Sister Alice. Who's to say you're not on her list?"

His posture straightens, his eyes suddenly focus, and he says evenly, "What are the chances she knows you're here?"

"Probably high. She's crafty."

"Oh, that's just great! Thank you so much!" He rushes down the hall, ducks into a room, and slams the door shut. A heavy piece of furniture slides from one side of the room to another and bangs against the door.

Dennis caresses my hand and says, "What's the backup plan when religion fails?"

"Stitches," I reply, as the pain of my wounds suddenly increase. Dennis helps me to stand, but when I straighten my knee a newly formed scab rips open and sends warm blood running down my leg. We take three steps toward the front door, but I'm too dizzy to continue.

"An ambulance should be here any minute," Father Desmond says. "Why don't you wait in the bathroom? Not to sound unkind, but you're staining the new carpet." Dennis guides me into a bathroom down the hall. I lean against the sink as he grabs two blue towels from a rack beside the shower. I press one to my shoulder while Dennis ties one around my knee. The priest watches us in the door frame and begins nibbling on his fingernails. "If Gail is responsible for the crimes, as you say, how would she know you're here?"

"I was fostered into her house," I reply, "we have a strange way of crossing paths." The barrel of a handgun suddenly appears aimed at his left temple, but he's unaware. The trigger is pulled before I can warn him. A terrible bang echoes through the room as his eyes fill with blood. Father Desmond drops to the floor like a string-cut marionette.

Gail steps over the priest while Dennis shoves me into the back wall. He stands with his arms outstretched to block her path. I try moving him aside, but he won't budge. "You can kill me in her place," Dennis says, "I'm not living without her!" Gail dispenses a remorseful sigh and fires two shots. One bullet rips straight through Dennis's forearm and cracks the tiled wall. The other hits his thigh and remains embedded. He collapses with a groan.

Gail points the gun at my face, winks, and pulls the trigger. The gun bangs and flashes. I expect a bullet to rocket through my face, but it shatters the window behind me. Gail cackles merrily and steadies the gun. I cringe in preparation of her next shot.

As Gail clicks back the firing hammer, Dennis kicks out his good leg against her left knee and buckles it inward. She crumples to the floor. I surge forward and pin her down with my knees on her elbows. She fires a shot that puts a hole in the bathtub, an indication she'll never give up, which destroys any compassion left within me.

While visions of all those she's claimed flash through my mind, I slap my left hand over Gail's face, grip her ridged larynx with my right hand, squeeze as hard as I can, and pull back with all my might. Skin and ligaments stretch and snap against my fist. Her shredded arteries pump streams of blood from a widening gorge. I stand with a final thrust, ripping her spongy throat free, and throw the moist clump onto her chest. She tries to pinch her neck together while the floor beneath her pools outward with foul blood. I should probably feel horror, but I feel nothing at all but relief.

When Gail releases her final gurgling breath, I instinctively begin to make the sign of the cross, but she deserves no such respect, so I drop my hand.

Father Vincent emerges from his room and glances fearfully down the hall. He perks up at the sight of Gail's wet corpse. His smile beams and a hand lands over his heart. "Oh, thank God," he says. "We're going to live!"

I'm not sure if any part of his heart or soul is reserved for the children who died because of what he did to Gail, but I do know they died because of him. Since God allowed children to perish under His watch, I'm forced to assume Father Vincent won't receive punishment for his role. I can't allow those kids to have died in vain. I pick up the revolver from Gail's puddle and say, "Unfortunately for you, Father, we all walk away from this with scars."

"I have no scars. You saw to that."

I fire a direct shot at his right knee. A hole tears through his pants while the floor behind him spatters with bloody chunks of bone. He howls as though he's completely sober.

"You'll acknowledge the victims whenever you kneel."

Father Vincent hobbles out of the bathroom. I turn to Dennis, who's sitting against a wall and holding a towel to his leg. I crumble beside him as sirens wail outside. Red and blue lights flash in the hallway. Dennis looks at me with a crooked smile that blends agony and joy. We lean our heads together and share a quiet, trembling smile of alleviation.

CHAPTER VIII

Using a crutch for the first time isn't easy, especially on the prowl. I struggle through a hospital corridor, searching for Dennis's room, which I'm told is on the same floor as mine. I'm careful not to make a noise that would cause the nurses to catch onto me, since I'm supposed to remain in bed, as evidenced by the pain that explodes from my mended wounds with every abrupt step I take. I'll have to use an arm sling and a knee apparatus for a while, but it's better than dying. Luckily, I'm not the only one to have survived in Gail's wake.

Barry suffered a massive coronary and is in intensive care recovering from a triple bypass. Unless he drastically changes his lifestyle and eating habits, chances are high he won't outlast the year. I can't say I'll miss him, but I appreciate that he tried to protect me.

Father Vincent didn't press charges on me for shooting him. Instead, he blamed the gunshot on

Gail. He said she tried to kill him because he refused to denounce God, thereby making himself a martyr. In front of reporters he tearfully thanked God for saving his life, and said he felt forlorn and heartbroken over the deceased children. Whether or not he feels anything at all is something I may never know. I don't plan on seeing him ever again.

Nathan will need a few days of observation for a severe concussion, and was placed under arrest for aiding and abetting a serial killer. Police believe he did more than drive Gail to the scenes, as they found bomb wiring in the garage that matched the remnants found in Sister Alice's bedroom. I find it hard to believe he had the composure to look me in the eye, since he had such a hand in the crimes. He will die in prison, alone and unforgiven.

As for Gail, the police were able to clear up some of the mystery, such as how she got to the rectory so fast. Apparently, we gave her a ride. When she fled from Barry's den she went straight into the hatchback of his SUV and wrapped herself in a blanket, probably knowing we'd drive away to seek help. Detectives found a file folder under the box spring of her mattress full of documents stolen from the rectory office. She had the locations of every child from the group home, a collection of addresses for families who have children under eighteen years of age, and a message to herself to stop Father Vincent's spread of Catholicism at its youngest source. Though I initially thought I would be punished for taking her life in such a gruesome manner, the police commended me for putting a stop to her horrific murder spree.

The police explained why only one cop showed up when I ran outside summoning them. Detective Morris had several officers staking out the house, as promised, but three separate fires were set to homes in our neighborhood, prompting them to external action. The police are still trying to figure out whether or not Gail and Nathan had anything to do with those incidents. I'm betting they did.

Social Services believe it's best to get me as far away from my past troubles as possible, and are shipping me off tomorrow to Pennsylvania. I'm told my latest foster family has an in-ground swimming pool and two playful dogs, and that I'll have a spacious room on an upper floor. I can't rejoice. I don't want to leave Dennis behind. I asked if he could come with me, but the suggestion was quickly denied. With nobody but a deranged Lori to take care of him, I have no idea what his future holds.

Knowing this is the last night I'll get to spend with Dennis, I find his room without anyone catching on.

He's laying on the bed with his mended leg in a suspension unit. The TV across from him is turned off, and he's staring outside at a moonlit sky. When my crutch squeaks against the polished floor, he looks at me with a welcoming smile, and shifts over slightly so I can climb in bed beside him. After I crawl under his arm, he holds me close so we can both fit on the slim mattress. He looks at me with moist eyes and runs a finger over my crucifix charm. "I'm surprised you haven't given up," he says. "You're the savior you were waiting for. Not God."

"It might take awhile before I get back to how I used to feel about Him," I say, "but I think He had two reasons for sending me to your house. You're my favorite one." I kiss him on the lips, then rest my head over his beating heart. Fearing I'll never hear it again, I try as hard as I can to not fall asleep.

I envision Dennis and me stepping off a silver bus in front of the Monroeville Mall. The building appears exactly as it does in his favorite movie, *Dawn of the Dead*. The parking lot is empty, except for numbered light poles, while truck trailers are parked in front of the entrances to barricade the bands of wandering corpses. None of the zombies bother us, as they seem content to dwell in a world where the worst has already happened.

We find our way into the mall by squeezing between a trailer and the glass door entryway. Luckily, one of the panels is unlocked. The power is on inside, which allows electronic window puppets to gyrate, a xylophone score to play over widespread speakers, and a clock tower to remind us that life will always go on despite the grimness of the outside world. We frolic hand in hand through the film locations (notably the arcade, bank, and supermarket), skate around the ice rink on our sneakers, and slide down the escalator divide at Penny's. We move with the merriment of living on our own in a place where evil has been obstructed.

Dennis eventually stops us on a wooden bridge that crosses a pond. When he wraps his arms around my stomach, I lean my backside against his hips. He points to a wooden wall that conceals a maintenance hall, and says close enough to dampen my ear, "That's the barricade the survivors built to keep the zombies out of the stairwell. We'll have to travel through the air ducts, but we'll live beyond there." He turns me around and puts his hands on my cheeks. "There's nothing to worry about anymore. We'll always be safe here." We then kiss with the passion of a couple allowed to grow up, and grow old, together.

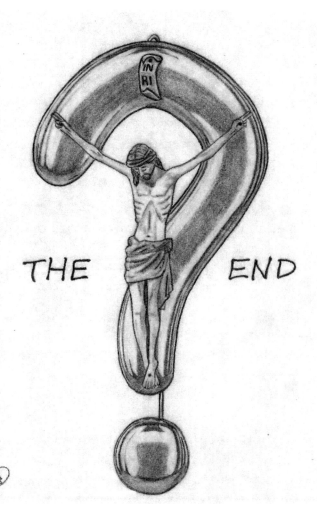

THE END

Acknowledgments

This book is dedicated to Alice Cooper. His songs and stage shows have rescued me from my lows and strengthened me in my highs. I've learned through his music that tackling the most serious subjects of life need not come across as heavy-handed. The grimness around us can be made entertaining through equal traces of awareness, shock, and humor.

A very special thanks to Kaylie Jones for her many years of patience and guidance. It's been a pleasure having her as a professor and friend.

Thank you to those who have read various incarnations throughout the years: Anastasiya Nabatova, Justin Kassab, Ashley Heffernan, Tara Reidy-Tosi, Gina Czark, Nina Solomon, Michelle Oster, Jennifer Andreas, and William Roberson.

A heartfelt thanks to Vincent Nasta, my tenth grade art teacher who taught me everything I needed to know about drawing in two seconds: "It's not a hand, Dave, it's shapes." Sadly, Mr. Nasta left us when the plane he was piloting at an air show crashed. He died doing what he loved most. We should all be so lucky.

Special thanks to *Fangoria*, the magazine that fueled my interest in horror. Interning for Tony Timpone and Michael Gingold during the summer of '99 was my first indication that dreams can indeed come true.

Last, but not least, thanks to *Mad Max: Fury Road*, the movie that sparked my soul back to life, pulled me up from the darkness, and led me to completing this story to the greatest of my abilities.

When his eyes fell upon *Fangoria* #82 during the spring of 1989, David Andreas became addicted to all things horror. The highlight of his life (so far) is having interned there during the summer of 1999. While amassing several thousand reviews for his own website, splattercritic.com, David received a Master of Fine Arts degree from LIU Southampton. Since 2007, he's been teaching English at several colleges, most notably St. Joseph's College in Patchogue, NY. *Angel of the Underground* is his debut novel, and the flagship publication of ODDITIES KJB, an imprint of Kaylie Jones Books for fans of character-driven horror and speculative fiction.

CPSIA information can be obtained
at www.ICGtesting.com
Printed in the USA
LVOW10s2003190218

567132LV00003BA/845/P